To

Val

Love & best wishes

Malcolm
x

Waiting in Line

Malcolm J Brooks

authorHOUSE

AuthorHouse™ UK
1663 Liberty Drive
Bloomington, IN 47403 USA
www.authorhouse.co.uk
Phone: 0800.197.4150

© 2017 Malcolm J Brooks. All rights reserved.

No part of this book may be reproduced, stored in a retrieval system, or transmitted by any means without the written permission of the author.

Published by AuthorHouse 04/29/2017

ISBN: 978-1-5246-8048-0 (sc)
ISBN: 978-1-5246-8047-3 (e)

Print information available on the last page.

Any people depicted in stock imagery provided by Thinkstock are models, and such images are being used for illustrative purposes only. Certain stock imagery © Thinkstock.

This book is printed on acid-free paper.

Because of the dynamic nature of the Internet, any web addresses or links contained in this book may have changed since publication and may no longer be valid. The views expressed in this work are solely those of the author and do not necessarily reflect the views of the publisher, and the publisher hereby disclaims any responsibility for them.

Dedication

This book is dedicated to all those people who carry out acts of random kindness. May what goes around, come around.

THANKS

My very great thanks go to Barbara, Bill, Carol, Christine, Colin and Margaret for all their hard work, kindness and patience. Their random acts of kindness come with very little reward.

The Thought

I kept having this thought. I wouldn't say it was a fantasy just a thought, but it kept popping into my brain. It was an illogical and stupid thought; one that had no sense at all, except I kept having it.

I had just celebrated my 18th birthday in the usual style of getting 'wasted' with friends. My parents, Amy and David, had given me a traditional celebration with relatives. Nowadays eighteen was the 'key to the door', the 'legal for anything' age, as opposed to twenty-one. 'Getting wasted' for those of you not familiar with the phrase means getting to the point where you remember nothing of what had happened to you or what you had to drink.

Many TV programmes have shown such revelry in places like Ibiza and Tenerife. It ended, as all these times do, with me throwing up at the side of the road and being carried home by my friends Joy, Rosie and Marci. They had been charged with my safe conduct back to my parents' house in Ferry Fryston.

The days that followed were dominated by feeling ill and stupid. I was still at school studying for my A levels, but

I wasn't really committed to them. I knew where my life was leading and the vocation I wanted to follow.

My certainty of what I was destined to become came from my 'special' talent or powers as I liked to call them. I had only met one person who had had my ability to do what I could do and that was back in 1605. Yes, that's what I said, 1605!

My special talent, for the want of a better word, was that I could travel back in time and I had done this twice in my life so far. Once, when I was eleven and later as a teenager. It had been very exciting but if I had to be honest, it had been very dangerous. This special power that I had enabled me to see both the living and, if the conditions were right, the dead.

It had all started when I was very young and I had met the ghost of a lady who had the same name as me, Eva. She had frequented my bedroom where she had died some fifty years earlier and she had visited me for as long as I could remember. Nobody in my family believed me. My sisters, Sharon and Sophie, regularly made fun of me when I tried desperately to describe the lady and the conversations we had.

Then one day, quite out of the blue, I met an elderly man called John. I say elderly but when you are eleven everybody over twenty is 'elderly'. I think he was in his late fifties when we first met and a little older when our second adventure in the 17th century took place.

John was different. In the first place, he believed me and my talk of seeing ghosts and I was desperate for somebody not to think that I was making it all up. What neither of us expected was that I could, with their permission, use the ghosts' 'corridors of transit' to travel back in time.

John was kind, gentle and full of humour and even though our great age gap might have impeded it, we became really good friends. Not of course in any sexual way but in the other kind of love that maybe a father might have for his daughter or even granddaughter.

The 17th century had, as I said, been very dangerous what with the Civil War and the 'Gunpowder plot', but we had survived and although John was in a heap of trouble when we returned for so called 'abducting' me, we both knew that that was far from the truth as Grace, the unfortunate policewoman who accidently came with us, could confirm.

Anyway, I digress. Back to my thought. Since to me my vocation in life was going to be in the ever widening antiques market, I could, with my time travel ability, bring things back from the past with little cost and from any period of time that I chose to select. All I needed was an appropriate ghost! Unlike my friends whose careers depended on A level exam success I felt that I had little to worry me, job-wise.

My weird thought was this; what would happen if, at my tender age of eighteen, I could arrange a chance meeting with John when he was about the same age. This really excited me. Yes, I had had a few teenage relationships of the 'fumbling' kind with boys. One boy that I had met at a dance was training to be a butcher, which for a burgeoning vegetarian had little chance of success. Another boy didn't pass the 'Dad test', mainly because of his tattoos and piercings! If John was the same kind of person at eighteen as he was when older then he was the man for me. Yes, a really stupid thought which even if I could come close to achieving it, it might alter his life and mine forever!

Eva

As the Easter of 2013 approached, I left all thoughts of meeting John to one side and concentrated on the forthcoming A level examinations. I had dropped AS physical education, the subject I really enjoyed, to focus on what I thought would be the best subjects to study as a potential time travelling antiques dealer. Mum and dad had never studied A levels and so only wanted what was best for me.

I had a few problems convincing the careers' teacher at my school that history, French and Spanish was a good combination.

"What do you want to do as a profession," she had asked, "after university?" She had added as an afterthought.

I really didn't think that I was destined for college or university. My special powers lay in other fields so to speak, rather than in the world of academia.

"I like all three subjects," I had lied, "but I am not sure I am good enough to go to college." This was much nearer the truth.

"They are three very difficult subjects for someone of your ability."

I had ignored this slight insult as it was most certainly true and my Year 12 exam results showed that at best I might get grade Ds in this year's exams. But my mind was set. I had, for some reason, been given special powers and, as my teachers had often said, I had to make the most of them even if they were not of the 'exam taking' kind. They were a pointer to what I was destined to become and I was going to do as the teachers had said and make the most of them!

I reasoned that history might give me the knowledge of which periods to visit to collect artefacts to sell. This, as it happens, wasn't particularly true, as history at A level was not about facts but more about reasoning. The French and Spanish I hoped would expand my market so to speak. Artefacts from France and Spain were widely mentioned on the TV's Antiques programmes.

The second trip that John and I took back to the 17th century in order to return Valentine, a young boy, to his mother Hester, had ended in me stealing some spoons from Coughton Manor which I sold for quite a handsome profit when I returned to 2008. This had sparked the idea of my future career.

I had tried my best at the subjects I had chosen but the oral examinations in French and Spanish gave me nightmares.

I was a confident sort of person but understanding the use of the subjunctive was beyond me and no matter how hard I tried, the predictions of grade Ds with a possible grade C if I was lucky were, in my opinion, just about right.

Waiting in Line

The exams started in May with the dreaded orals but my torture was over by mid-June so I could return to my thought.

Most of my friends were plotting a holiday away in the sun to Magaluf, but I declined because I had my mind set on a trip of a very different kind! It dawned on me as I lay in the sunshine of a beautiful June morning that I had very little to go on in my goal of meeting John. What did I actually know about John as a teenager?

If he was about sixty in 2008 then, in 1967, he would have been eighteen or nineteen. I knew that he must have gone to college or university because he became a teacher, but that was about it. It must have been a northern university because he never spoke about living in the south or midlands and, like me, he had a very Yorkshire accent.

OK, so in order to get to 1966 or 1967 I needed an appropriate ghost. The way it had worked in 2006 and 2008 was that I had used the ghost of someone who had died or been born on the date to which I wanted to return. Yes, I know it sounds complicated but the 'corridors of transit' through which I could travel were only related to the birth date and death date of the person I was using. I had to find the ghost of someone who had died around the year 1967 or had been born then and subsequently died.

If you are still with me at this point you will appreciate that this wasn't going to be easy, but I had plenty of time on my hands after my exams had finished.

My first port of call was probably to visit my hometown library. They had, I was certain, microfiche files of people involved in the various censuses that had been taken over the years. My father had used it to trace parts of his 'family tree' and had taken me along for my technical knowledge! He had said that he was old and unsure of what to do with modern technology. I tried to tell him that microfiche had been around for ages but he wouldn't believe me!

And then it struck me!! I didn't know his full-name! Yes, OK John was his first name but John what?

That night, I laid in bed pondering my options of achieving my ridiculous goal and cursing myself for knowing so little about my innocent victim in all this when she appeared and of course, that was the answer!

Eva was John's grandmother and surely she knew everything I needed to know.

"Hello Eva," the way I always started our conversations. It was a bit formal I know but she was a lady of reverence and any other method of greeting, I felt, would have been inappropriate.

"Hello Eva," came the response and we had often both smiled at the symmetry of this well-versed greeting routine.

"I've got something to ask you." I said unsure as to how I could reasonably approach the subject.

"What is it my dear Eva?"

"Your grandson's name. What is it?" It came out a little more abruptly than I had anticipated.

"Which one? I have six."

"You're teasing me, Eva. You know which one!"

"You mean John?"

"Yes, John."

"Well, let me think. It's John." Nanna Eva had a sense of humour!

"Very funny. What is his surname?"

"I do need to think this time. Things don't quite come as easy when you're my age."

"What age would that be Eva?"

"What year is it?"

"2013."

"Well, I was born in 1884 so that would make me, let me see, that makes me one hundred and twenty-nine, I think!"

"Ok, we have established your age, what about John?"

"Oh, he's sixty-four."

"OK, very funny."

"I love it when you say 'OK.' It's such a strange word."

"My mum says 'okay dokey' but I haven't a clue why, or where the words come from."

"It sounds like the way an American would say it."

"Yes, I suppose it does. Anyway, can we get back to John's surname?"

"His full name is John Albert Evans. John was his uncle's name and Albert was his grandfather's name."

"Your husband's name?"

"No, on his father's side."

"I need to know a bit more about him. What college he went to and any girlfriends he had."

"That's a strange request. Why don't you go and ask him? You know where he lives."

It's true I did. He hadn't moved too far away but I didn't think I could ask him the questions I wanted to because he might want to know why I needed to know.

"It's a little too personal and I'm not sure John would like my reasons for wanting to know."

"Do I get the reasons?" Eva asked.

So I told her my thought. She looked, for the first time that I could remember, disapprovingly at me.

"Are you sure that you can meddle in his life like that? Is it fair to him?"

"No, I suppose not but what harm can it do?"

"It depends on what you are planning to do when you meet him."

"I haven't really thought too much about it, other than it would be nice to meet him when we are both the same age."

"It's dangerous Eva. You could alter his life and all that happens after."

"What do you mean?"

"Meddling in things you cannot possibly understand."

"I didn't change anything on the two occasions John and I went back to the 17th century. We were very careful not to."

"Can you be certain you changed absolutely nothing?"

"No, I suppose not. Maybe we did in some small way."

"I must leave now. Things to do. By the way, John went to college in the city of Durham. Goodbye little Eva."

And with that she was gone, leaving me to ponder her warning about the thought that I had had.

John

I'd failed. There were no other words for it. I'd failed from the moment I had finished my exams. I knew my dreams were over. I cried real tears, there were no crocodiles around.

When the results came out, I cried again because they were just as bad as I had expected and I had failed to get into the college that I had really wanted. Yes, of course, there were other options, other colleges. I had a half-hearted plan B, and a plan C and D for that matter but I felt, for the first time that I was a real failure. I had been predicted all grade As and although I thought that my teachers were a little too optimistic, the two grade Bs I needed to get into the college in Durham were obtainable, but I had failed miserably to get them.

OK, I had lots of sympathetic words from my lovely parents and girlfriend Ann, but after the results came out I moped about wondering what option to take. A college down south or in Wales or even to Blackburn in Lancashire were all possibilities.

Even my headmaster tried to pull in a few favours from friends of his on my behalf and I had thought that he didn't like me too much. He had actually phoned around on the morning of the results to see if the lowly grades I had obtained could get me in somewhere. The college in Blackburn that I mentioned earlier was all as a result of his endeavours. Allegedly, there were lots of holes in Blackburn, Lancashire according to the Beatles, but I had never been there to find out.

I've never been good with choices that are thrust upon me. I was a planner but in my own time and up to now most things had gone to plan. OK, I failed my driving test but I just saw that as a blip, my foot slipped off the brake in an emergency stop. Just one of those things!

Ann had successfully got into her first choice college in the Midlands and was excited about going. I was depressed, not clinically of course, but seeing things in a 'half-empty' sort of way.

Fate, however, is a strange beast. It kicks you around like a pinball machine. Sometimes you are hitting all the right places and then you descend into the gutter.

"John! John! There's a letter for you from Durham." I awoke to the sound of my mother's excited voice and I could hear her footsteps coming up the stairs to the bedroom that I shared with my grandfather.

"John, there's a letter for you," came the repeated statement of fact. Half-heartedly I dragged myself up from my slumbers just as mum entered the bedroom. Knocking on doors wasn't a tradition in our house. Reluctantly, I took the letter from her and started to open it. I could imagine what it would say, words like 'sorry', 'failed' and the slightly optimistic 'try again next year' and 'best of luck'.

It started. 'Dear John'. I had to smile. I thought 'Dear John' letters were about relationship break-ups. Maybe this was, in a funny sort of way, just such a break-up.

I read on:

'We would like to offer you a place at the University of Durham to do…….' The rest was just a blur, apart from the end bit. 'If you would like to take up this offer ……..'

"They want me, they want me!" I screamed. I jumped out of bed and hugged my mother so tightly that she squealed.

EVA

It was decision time. Was I going through with my ridiculous plan, and more importantly, what was the plan?

So I now knew the college John attended and approximately the year. It was probably 1966 or maybe 1967. The question was 'how would I get there?' Strangely enough travelling to 1966 from 2013 seemed less of a problem than getting from my hometown to Durham. Since I was 11 years old I had travelled back in time and I knew the process I had to go through. Sadly, it did involve life and death. The 'corridor of transit' that allowed me to travel back in time involved, in the first instance, me finding someone who had died. Using the ghost of this person, I could return to their year of birth or their year of death. Unfortunately, I had no control over where I would arrive in those times since it was determined by the place where they were born or where they died.

So in a way my task was simple? As I have said, I needed to locate the ghost of a person who had died or was born in 1966 or 1967. I do realize that this statement, to those who do not have my special powers, seems far from simple, but the task of getting anywhere in England in 1967 would present problems. First of all, I had no money from that pre-decimalised time and I did not have a clue about the transport system at that time. Since my birth in 1995 I have known about mobile phones, laptop computers and credit cards, none of which were available as far as I knew, in the 1960s. This meant that some research was necessary.

The results of my exams were due out in August so I did have some time after they had finished to research my plan of action. Firstly, to get some 1960s money.

JOHN

The complete shock of receiving a letter accepting me and my lowly grades took some time to sink in. I had taken a holiday job at a local factory and was working a rotation of shifts; 'days, afternoons and the dreaded nights'. So this did occupy my mind somewhat.

The rest of the time, apart from seeing Ann, was spent preparing to leave home. I made a list of the sort of things that I would need, a knife, a fork, spoons, a cup and a sherry glass. Why I had thought I needed the latter was, in hindsight, a mystery but I bought two!

My mother was just as excited as I was at the prospect of me going away to college. Whether it was the excitement of getting rid of me I never found out, but maybe she was just excited for me. With items bought and things packed, I boarded the train in early October bound for the hundred or so mile journey north.

My life was about to change irreversibly. I was to leave my polluted, industrial town in the West Riding of Yorkshire, where the washing came in soot-ridden after being 'on the line' for any period of time, to a small city which, although it was also in the middle of a mining area, had a 'clean' feel to it.

My lodgings for the next year were in Shincliffe Hall, in a small village just outside the city boundaries. It appeared at first sight to be an old farm with a courtyard that had been converted into rooms for twenty-eight 'fresher' students.

To reach Shincliffe Hall from the main road it was necessary to walk up a lane with wonderful hedges and fields on both sides and eventually through a small wood, a distance of about a mile. The Hall had a Victorian feel to it, as if I was being transported back in time. The other twenty-seven students were an eclectic mix of people, the likes of which I had never encountered before.

The first thing that marked me out as being different was the way I spoke. It soon became apparent that many of the others found my Yorkshire accent funny and it was a constant source of great amusement for most of them. In truth I got used to the choruses of 'shut t' door' each time I encouraged somebody to close the door to the Common Room. Fortunately, if I have any good points in my personality, one was simply the ability to laugh at myself. Of course, I soon learned to give as good as I got and my mimicry of different accents improved as the year went along.

Many of the students were from rich families and had attended expensive public schools, but they were still human with all the frailties that eighteen year olds possess. The other thing that seemed apparent to me at the start was that the vast majority of these boys were far more intelligent than me and unlike me they must have achieved the A level grades expected of them.

However, I quickly developed a work ethic and soon got into a routine that involved attending all lectures and frequent visits to the library. The lectures were scary with over a hundred students present and little time to scribble notes that the lecturer kept writing on (and rubbing off) the distant blackboard.

There wasn't much time for a social life either. In any case I had a girlfriend about 150 miles away. Sport took up the rest of my time and there were hardly any students of the female gender in the classes I attended.

I shared a large room with a boy called Jim who came from a small private school and lived near Cambridge. We were very different and had totally opposite backgrounds but we got on well and had a similar sense of humour. What was that saying, 'the prettiest thing you can wear is a smile' and smile we did when we weren't studying. He studied classics which was a total mystery to me or as you might say, 'all Greek to me'!

Durham had fifty-four public houses but with a ratio of five male students to one female, the most intriguing aspect of all this happened at the entrance to the Student Union building, Dunelm House.

The building on the banks of the River Wear was host to some great pop groups of the sixties; Procol Harum, The Nashville Teens, Long John Baldry, Manfred Mann, The Tremeloes, The Crazy World of Arthur Brown and many

Waiting in Line

others. However, the rule was that any local, non-student person could only gain entry to the dances or bars by being signed in by a student. This was manna from heaven for many of the male students, as consequently every night, particularly on Fridays and Saturdays, there was a long line of available girls wishing to get into the building. Male students would walk up and down the line of girls, perusing the 'talent' on offer before selecting one to escort into the dance or bar. Of course, what happened once these girls were inside depended on the attraction being reciprocated.

Eva

I made a list of the things I needed for my trip back to the 60s. Few people knew of my special powers or my plans to revisit the past for the third time.

Joy was my best friend from school. She was one of those people who always saw the positive in everything, always smiling and in helpful mode. She was the kind of friend you needed when you were unsure of what you are doing.

"Money," she said, "from the right time and clothes from the period too."

She never questioned that what I was doing was mad and that I must be deranged when I told her of my plans. She had been one of the few who I had allowed to see at firsthand what I could see. My powers allowed anyone touching me to see what I could see, which in my world meant that they too could see people that had died. I had, perhaps after slightly too much to drink, introduced Joy to Nanna Eva, I am not too sure that Nanna Eva was too pleased about this introduction as she said later it was as if I was showing off whilst under the influence of alcohol. She was right but despite the drink, Joy was very respectful and remarkably unmoved by what she saw, maybe the drink did have an influence on her behaviour.

It was confusing for Joy to understand my world of ghosts and 'corridors of transit'. It seemed straightforward to me, if ever time travel could be seen as straightforward. As well as the dates and places of birth and death of the ghosts that I could visit, there were also their 'special places' that they chose to frequent. I never quite followed how this worked despite Nanna Eva's many attempts to explain it. As I had discovered on my last trip into the past, I could see ghosts shortly after the person had died whilst, as I learned, they were in a place called Limbo. I always rationalised that this was during the time it took God to decide what to do with them!

"Oh, and what about shoes?" Joy's words brought me back to earth and she was being as practical as ever, "and no digital watch just one of those clock-faced things." She finished her statement with such a strange, obvious description!

"Good thinking, Joy." I confirmed, but she was on a roll.

"No mobile phone, no laptop or computer of any sort!"

"Don't think I was going to take my laptop."

Joy was unfazed and continued as she had started. "The difficulty would be in not talking about things that have not happened or things that haven't been invented."

"I have done this sort of thing before you know." I complained.

"And did you make any mistakes then?"

"Well, yes a couple of times but nothing I couldn't talk my way out of. I'm a lot older now."

"What stupid things did you say?"

I hesitated. "I did finish up once having to say that I rode a horse to Spain! I forgot there were no planes in the 17th century and people didn't travel abroad much and I stupidly said I'd been on holiday to Spain. Fortunately, I didn't mention 'by plane'".

Joy giggled.

"I was only eleven so I did make the occasional faux pas, but John usually managed to dig me out of the hole I got myself into, except occasionally, he let me stew when it didn't matter so much, like the time I mentioned cars and traffic lights!"

"What was he like, this John?"

"Really kind and understanding in a 'granddad' type of way. We had a great sense of humour with each other. Like me, he was quick witted with sarky comments. Occasionally, he got grumpy but he was very protective towards me. At times I had to hide what I was doing from him, like when Robin and I blew up a Royalist cannon."

"That's amazing. I wish I could come with you. What was Robin like?"

"He was 14 and I was 11, so I fancied him! He was really good-looking and posh. His father was a Member of Parliament and was a Roundhead."

"Always sounds funny to me 'Roundhead'. Everybody has a round head!"

"Yes, it sounded funny to me too. Would you really like to come with me? It might be a bit dangerous."

"How would travelling back to the 1960s be dangerous? Hardly Civil War time was it? But travelling back to that time to see what it was like sounds fantastic."

"If we aren't careful they might think that we are strange or even spies if we were to talk about 2013 and what we did."

"How long are you going for?"

"Not sure. As long as it takes."

"As long as what takes?"

"Until I meet John when he is eighteen years old!"

"What if you don't like him? People change you know."

"Yep, I suppose they do. It's a chance I have to take. I can come back any time I wish if I can find the right ghost!"

"How did it all start, this ghost thing?"

"I first met Nanna Eva when I was about six. You know that she was John's grandmother. I didn't know who she was at first but once I'd met John, he told me who she was."

"Could he see her too?"

"No, not without my help but he just believed me when I told him about this ghostly lady I had met, nobody else believed me, and we worked out who it was sometime later."

"Hairstyle!" Joy screamed.

"What?"

"That red tinted hairstyle of yours might not look right. You'll have to have your hair done to fit in. We should be able to look on the Internet to find out what the girls wore and what their hair looked like."

"Good idea, we'll do it tomorrow. Any other ideas Joy?"

John

After 'fresher's week', which in many ways was not the ideal introduction to the hard-working life of a university, things settled down into a routine. It started slowly at first as any new way of life does but then picked up pace. It was clear to me early on that I was nowhere near being as bright as the other students on my course. I tried to make up for my lack of brainpower with frequent visits to the library to try and make some sense of the copious notes (sometimes inaccurate) that I had taken during the mass lectures.

These mass lectures with over 120 students in them entailed the lecturer writing from left to right on a large blackboard with little in the way of explanation, followed by his dreaded blackboard duster act of writing with his right hand and removing earlier bits with his left. If you weren't quick enough it meant that you missed large sections of the relevant notes which either you begged from a fellow student or made it up the best you could from textbooks!

Having a girlfriend 150 miles away in some way was helpful, however with my fellow course members being predominantly male there was little chance of talking to the fair sex.

Sport took up what little leisure time I had, although I did visit home occasionally by hitching lifts in all manner of vehicles. My family did not possess a car, so on return journeys I had to catch a bus to the nearest point on the A1 north and start my 100 or so mile hitchhike from there.

Bruce and June were a partnership from their school days and although June was at an all-female college, they were on the same course as I was. June originated from Toronto and was what can only be described as a live wire. Bruce was more reserved and assured. He seemed much more mature than I was, and that may in part be down to the fact that he had attended a public school, which in some way had moulded his character, but clearly the school had not had the same effect on June!

It was Bruce who encouraged me to buy a Capri motor scooter for the princely sum of £13. I was no mod or rocker for that matter but since Bruce had a similar mode of transport, the idea was that we could 'easy rider' our way to lectures in tandem, so to speak.

The £13 doesn't sound much but out of a grant of £360 which had to account for all my outgoings, it was probably an expenditure I could have done without. However, the purchase was made and for a couple of weeks, things went well.

The first lecture always began at 9am so an 8.30 or so departure from the Hall was the target.

On a cold and frosty November morning we met as usual at 8.30 in the courtyard. Once out of the wooded section, the lane leading to the main Durham road was, for the want of a better word, a tunnel. It was about a mile in length and had high hedges on both sides, maybe a cars-width apart. You took a deep breath at the start and hoped that nobody was coming the other way. Usually in the mornings it wasn't a problem as everybody left the Hall and made their way down to the main road. Occasionally, the odd pedestrian and bicycle made it problematic, but this crisp winter morning had none of these obstacles.

Strangely, Bruce let me go first, an unusual occurrence but maybe he had a premonition of what was to follow. The first section was uphill through the trees before hitting the 'hedge' section, which was a steep downhill with a sharp right-hand bend around which you couldn't see a thing.

Maybe I was travelling a little faster down the hill than was appropriate for that particular morning, but as I turned round the bend I saw it! How on earth it got there still remains a mystery to me, but right in front of me, sitting across the road was a cow!

The next thing I know, I am flying through the air and instinct made me put down my right hand to break my fall, in fact the only things it broke were my hand and arm. It sounds a bit selfish but how the stupid cow felt about the incident I haven't a clue. Being hit at 30 mph by a piece of metal must have hurt and had consequences for the poor animal.

I never knew exactly what happened to the poor cow as eventually I was taken to the local County Hospital where it was confirmed that I had broken my arm and a number of fingers as well. The rugby season was over for the foreseeable future.

My precious £13 bike was unrepairable and fortunately for Bruce, he had time to come to a skidding halt with no damage to either him or his bike. Such is fate!

The other cuts and bruises I received healed quickly but the two alterations to my life were that I had to walk the two miles or so to lectures and had to learn to write with my undamaged left hand as my right arm had a pot on it with bandages around my fingers.

Neither alteration to my life was welcome, but Christmas was approaching and I had a couple of exams before the holiday started on which to focus my attention and I had to do well in both of them.

Eva

"Where you going to get money from Eva?" Was Joy's question. "It will be expensive to buy it from the shop selling old coins to collectors."

"It will, but I have a bit of an idea." I replied.

"What, steal it?"

"Sort of. I thought I'd make a visit to the 60s before we go and sell some stuff from nowadays."

"Won't that be slightly dangerous and against the law?"

"I don't think there's a law against time travellers selling stuff from the future."

"Aren't you better going even further back in time and nicking things to sell as antiques in the 60s?" Joy was great at offering solutions!

"That's an idea. Wouldn't be as suspicious as trying to sell a mobile phone!"

"They wouldn't work anyway because there would be no satellites to transmit the texts and calls."

"True, I might get locked up as a spy or something."

"Who would be the spies back then?"

"Suppose it would be the Russians. Anyway back to getting money. What could I sell that I can get lots of and that wouldn't raise any suspicions?"

"Fags!" Joy suggested.

"What?"

"Cigarettes. They must have been smoked a lot then when people didn't know as much about the harm they caused."

"Oh yeah, right. I can take loads of cigs back saying 'smoking kills' on the packet. They'd be really popular!" I loved teasing her but at least she was coming up with ideas, even if they were slightly impractical.

"Oh, I see what you mean!"

"There must be something. How about DVDs?"

"Not invented." Joy replied.

"CDs?"

"Nope. Not invented."

"How do you know?"

"Cos I went on the Internet to see what was around then."

"And?"

"Well, cassette tapes, yo-yos, hula-hoops." Joy listed the possibilities.

"You mean those crisps shaped like a polo mint?"

"No, silly. Hoops you dance with, to keep you fit and your stomach trim."

"They kept fit with hoops. That's weird!"

"I've seen them on a history programme. They used to put them round their waists and wiggle to keep them spinning for as long as they could."

"You're having me on, Joy."

"No, I'm not. Anyway, what about cosmetics? We know lots about them. There are plenty of different things that we can take and you can pretend that it's a new brand."

"That's meddling with history Joy and I try not to do that. You are robbing somebody of a creation they won't be able to make."

"This is hard. What sort of craze was there in the late sixties apart from hula hoops that we can get hold of cheaply and sell for a big profit?"

"We?"

"Oh, I've been meaning to ask you, Eva. Can I come too? We could help each other out and I know from what you said, I could go with you into the past."

"Yes, but it's dangerous, Joy. Things can go wrong, like they did with John the first time we went back, and for poor Grace the second time."

"What happened to them?"

"Well, John finished by taking a baby from the 17th century back to his wife Ann and by getting arrested for kidnapping two small children."

"Two small children?"

"Yes, I was the other one!"

"And Grace?"

"Ah, poor Grace. She was a young policewoman who John was physically attached to by handcuffs when I transported him back to 1605, and sadly she suffered horrible burns in an explosion. We did get her back, but she had to undergo lots of skin grafts."

"But please can I come with you? Life has been boring since we finished the exams and all my other mates have gone to Ibiza, clubbing it."

"Why didn't you go with them?"

"Dad wouldn't let me. Says he'd seen a programme on telly and knows what goes on and 'no daughter of mine', you know the sort of protective 'Dad thing'."

"It shows he cares, I suppose."

"Suppose so."

"I'd better do some more research on the sixties I guess. See you later."

Party at the Dun Cow Inn

Birthday parties at the pub in the centre of Durham called the Dun Cow Inn were a common occurrence. Some students were older than those of us who had come straight from school, and allegedly more mature. From my observations in November, this was most definitely not true.

Geoff was a public schoolboy from Haberdasher Aske School in London. He had taken time out travelling before university so was a bit older than the rest of us. He was a good-looking, intelligent, well-spoken student and an all-round nice person (nice in the nicest sense of the word!). Sickening really! It was Geoff's 21st birthday one Sunday in November and as usual, virtually all of us went to the pub. We had established a friendship through playing rugby for the University.

As my winger, he would often scream at me 'John, pass it now' and as he possessed a real turn of speed, it was a sensible option. I thought I was fast but he could easily outpace me. We were a good combination both on and off the field and since he studied economics and was older than me, I felt that he would be a good influence on me in my first year away from home. At least that's what I thought as we walked down to the pub on that cold Sunday evening.

The evening started in a typical fashion of rounds of drinks with Geoff having whisky chasers as well as his pints. I knew my limit and as unofficial guardian of Geoff's well-being, I dipped out after round six. I wasn't a wealthy student and as a supposed rugby player, I was lightweight when it came to drinking.

I lost count of how many drinks Geoff had had but he seemed coherent and in good spirits. Some students, I had noticed, got depressed or solemn as they drank more, but not Geoff.

The drinking games were in full swing. 'Fizz-Buzz' was a game which was mathematical, or more accurately arithmetical, in its nature. A circle was formed and the 'drink master' started with a loud 'one', the person to his left said 'two', the next person said 'Fizz', next came 'four' and then 'Buzz' for the fifth person. After that any multiple of three or five or any number containing a three or five was either a 'Fizz' (3) or 'Buzz' (5). In the case of the number 15, if it got that far without error, was 'Fizz Buzz'. The person who was first to make a mistake was 'enforced' to drink three fingers of beer by the 'drink master'.

Even in my slightly tipsy state my arithmetic ability was reasonable, but not so Geoff's. He made a fair number of mistakes and drank a fair amount of alcohol but still seemed OK. The truth of the matter was that there was a simple correlation between the amount of alcohol drunk and the number of mistakes made.

As the night progressed, Geoff seemed fine; lucid and happy but seemingly not overly drunk. However, I was about to learn a few lessons about the abuse of alcohol which up to that point, I am ashamed to say, I knew nothing about.

We decided to leave the pub and walk back to our room in Hatfield College. I remember feeling quite sober and opened the door in order to allow Geoff to leave first. He shouted his drunken thanks to all who had made the evening so good and without any clue as to what he might do next, suddenly as the fresh air hit him he shot off at full speed towards Elvet Bridge and the city centre.

"I've got a 9 o'clock economics lecture," he shouted as he raced down the road. Even with all that alcohol inside him he could travel fast. Playing on the wing for Durham University Rugby team meant that he was swift over at least sixty yards.

I gave chase. He was still shouting about being late for his early morning lecture as he put more and more distance between himself and the pursuing chasers. Of course, we did eventually catch up with him when he was being physically sick over the side of the bridge, increasing the liquid flow of the River Wear. 'Psychedelic yodelling' as it was called was never a pleasant sight, be it you or someone else. I remember feeling sorry for the fish that might possibly feast on the contents of Geoff's stomach. Why does it always look like carrots in cream sauce?

Before the night was finally over, I learned my second lesson! We managed to get Geoff back to his room. He was still very jovial and thanking everyone for being so kind despite his self-inflicted illness. He said that the world kept spinning, in fact we had to wait some time for the door to his room to come around again before he would allow us to step through it!

Sadly, as most people are aware, the 'aeroplane spin' precedes 'psychedelic yodelling'. As he lay there on his bed, still grinning inanely and thanking everyone and joking, the spin must have started again. In one swift movement he jumped from the bed, pushed past me and was violently sick in the small hand basin that all our rooms possessed.

And there, I thought as I later spooned out those large deposits from the sink that were too big to go down the 'plughole', was my second lesson of the night. Never, under any circumstances, allow people to be sick in a sink and always have a bucket at hand!

JOY

"I've got it!" I screamed at Eva as we met to discuss our travel plans.

"Got what?"

"Got how we can make money in 1967!"

"But we've thought of all the things we can sell and either we can't get enough of them or like the Rubrik's Cube, they weren't invented in 1967 and I don't meddle with history."

"Don't you remember what that general studies teacher said and we thought it was stupid?"

"He said a lot of stupid stuff. What bit precisely?"

"Information is power!"

"Yeah, I didn't quite follow that. Seemed even more stupid than usual."

"Read that! I got this book from my dad. It's all about the twentieth century. It does it year by year and month by month. Giving all the important things that happened. Look at this!"

I handed dad's very large and hefty book to Eva.

"Millennium 20th Century Day by Day? What use is this except as a doorstop?"

Waiting in Line

"Look what it says for April 1967."

"Ali stripped of title for refusing draft?" She read out loud. "Who is Ali?"

"Not that bit stupid. The bit below it!"

"Winner of Grand National at 100-1."

"Yes, that's the one."

"I don't understand what you are getting at Joy."

"Well, according to the book on April 8th, a rank outsider called Foinavon won the Grand National at Liverpool at 100-1. If we can get a couple of pounds of 1967 money and put it on that horse, we win £200. Ta rah!"

"Wow, you're a genius, Joy. Information is money!"

"Not so stupid after all, that general studies teacher!"

"Ah," Eva's face suddenly lost its smile. "Neither of us have been into a bookies before and aren't we too young?"

"You're right about not having done it before, but we are both eighteen and can gamble if we want to and I can't see them not wanting to take money from two gullible girls betting on a rank outsider. Lots of people bet on the Grand National, even if they have never bet before."

"It's certainly a possibility but we need to do a bit more research."

"Ask your dad, Eva. He gambles a bit doesn't he?"

"You must be joking. He'd kill me if he thought I was gambling." "Typical man. It's OK for them to bet but not for us women. In some ways we are still in the dark ages!"

"Let me just read that bit in the book again."

"I'll read it to you Eva, just in case you get stuck on the big words."

"You cheeky mare." Eva smiled.

"A pile-up of riderless, fallen and baulked horses at the 23rd fence turned the Grand National into near farce today and allowed Foinavon, a rank outsider ridden by John Buckingham to thread his way through to romp home to win the world's most famous steeplechase at the staggering price of 100-1."

"This means we need the ghost of a person born in 1967 but it has to be on or before April 8th." Eva confirmed as if she knew that I knew what she was talking about.

"You know all about that sort of thing, Eva. I leave all that 'ghostly thing' up to you. I don't know how your powers work."

"In one sense it's simple really. It seems that when people die they go into a place called 'Limbo' whilst decisions are made as to their final resting place. Then some people have a choice of places they can frequent and these places seem to be linked to their place of birth and death and on occasions they are linked to a special place, special to their lives that is."

"How long are people in Limbo?"

"It seems to vary. Henry was there for ages and so was Mary but with others it's been as little as a week."

"Who were Henry and Mary?"

"Just two people that sadly were killed in the English Civil War. They helped John and me get through a very difficult time."

"You are very brave. I'm not sure I would be so brave even if I had your powers. Tell me more about what we are going to do."

"Are you absolutely certain that you want to come with me? It's not all positive. We may have to deal with some pretty awful sights."

"How come?"

"We need to find someone who has died and what they look like in death is not always pretty."

"So what has to happen for us to go back to 1967?"

"It's not easy to be so specific. I need to research people who were born around March or early April of 1967 who have recently died."

"Wow, that's not going to be so easy. A really difficult problem to solve."

"Maybe too difficult, but we need to keep trying to find someone. One possibility is to keep looking at the deaths column in the local papers."

"How old must they be?"

"Well, it's 2013 and they were born in 1967, so that's 46 years-old."

"A bit young for someone to die."

"True. Makes the job a little more difficult."

"What other things do we need?" I asked her.

"Appropriate 1967 clothes and shoes. We'll need a place to stay so we need to find out how much that will cost us per week."

"How long are we staying?"

"That's a point. Haven't really thought about it."

"Maybe, we should put £4 on Foinavon."

"Could do."

"Well, we've made some progress." I concluded.

"I've got to go and babysit for Sophie. Mum and dad are going to the cinema tonight. See you laters," and off Eva went.

I opened dad's book and started to read once more through the events of 1967. I was really excited at the prospect of improving my sad, humdrum life by a visit to another time. I reasoned that the more I knew about that time the better we could handle our adventure.

Some poor man called Donald Campbell had died trying to break the world water-speed record on Coniston Water. His body hadn't been found and frogmen had called off their search for his body. Some American astronauts had been killed on a launch pad and there was a war in Vietnam, wherever that was.

There was an interesting section on 'flower power' and I could only imagine from the picture what an acceptable dress code might be. Articles on a ship that had run aground down near the Scilly Isles, another war, this time between Israel and the Arab states, a group called the Beatles which my granddad had once mentioned had lost their manager Brian Epstein and in November they had had to devalue the pound, whatever that meant!

JOHN

It wasn't fair. I wasn't exactly sure who it 'wasn't fair' to. It was a statistic and a rule that made it unfair and that was a certainty.

The statistic was that for every one female at the University there were five males. The rule in question was that to get into the Student Union for one of its many highly rated discos, the local girls had to stand in line, like in some sort of cattle market, waiting to be selected by a male student in order to be escorted into the building. Each student was allowed to sign in one guest, provided they showed their student card.

So every Friday, Saturday and sometimes Sunday night, an array of pretty local girls stood in a line waiting to be selected. I could only assume that some never did and stood there all evening long.

I guess it wasn't fair to these teenage girls to be looked upon in this way every weekend but it was even less fair on the local lads who didn't have the 'pulling power' of getting the girls into the disco.

Anyway, what seemed to me even worse was that in the month of October and throughout the winter these girls braved some arctic conditions in their scantily clad attire of miniskirts and short-sleeved tops, hoping to be selected and taken into the warmer climes of the student disco.

The reason why the girls were prepared to endure such hardship, I could only assume, was that the dances attracted famous pop groups who all had records, at some time recently, in the charts and the local girls were desperate to get close to these celebrities with also the possibility of bagging themselves a student boyfriend.

On this particular Saturday night, the star attraction was Long John Baldry who as yet had not had a chart hit but was a singer that all girls seemed to like. Although my hand and arm were still painful and in pot, I decided that I needed a night away from studying. As I strolled along Dunelm Bridge across the River Wear towards the Union building I could see a very long line of girls awaiting selection. I had a long-standing girlfriend so my criteria for selection wasn't perhaps the usual one adopted by most male students.

'The kindest eyes' was my first and foremost criteria, although this wasn't always obvious when walking down the line. Being of a semi-shy disposition myself with my terrible acne complexion I often sensed that the girls didn't want to be selected by me, just in case they got stuck with me inside, particularly with my arm heavily bandaged. Maybe a potential nurse might take pity on me?

This evening I chose a very nervous-looking, slim fair-haired girl for whom it may have been her first queuing

Waiting in Line

experience. With a tap on her shoulder with my good hand, the sign that she had been chosen, she dutifully followed me into the building to be signed in. I suppose it was the duty of the student signing the person in to be responsible for their behaviour for that evening but this never seemed to be the case.

"Thank you very much," she said, "is it OK if I wait here for my friend?"

This often happened as groups of girls were on a night out together and had to wait for all of them to be 'selected' before entering the place where tonight Long John Baldry would be performing.

"Of course it is." I replied. "I might see you later," and with that the brief encounter came to an end.

I needed to descend three flights of wide steps to get to the nearest bar to the dance floor and I stopped after the second flight to look at the sports' noticeboard that gave a list of fixtures and teams for each of the various sports. With my hand injury I had had to withdraw from the second team match against Sunderland and had dutifully crossed out my name and it had been replaced with the name of the person promoted from the third team. The teams for today's match were still there and a message 'Won 24-10' had been scrawled over it.

As expected, on entering the bar, I bumped into lots of other rugby players and one particular friend who was also called John and who was at the same college as me. He was from Cardiff and was a brilliant player who unfortunately played in the same position as me. He had gone straight into the first team as a fresher after playing for and captaining the Welsh Schoolboys' team and playing for Cardiff. Not only was he an outstanding player but a really good-looking lad with dark hair and a spotless complexion. Above all, he was a really nice lad with no airs or graces that you might expect with all that talent and success. Sadly, not all the players in the first team were like this!

"Hi John. Did you win?" I asked.
"Only just boyo. 11-9. And you?"
I held up my hand. "With this?"
"Oh yes, sorry I forgot about the cow incident!"
"It says on the board that the second team won 24-10. Did you manage to score?"
"Just the one!"

I didn't really need to ask. I reckoned my sidestep was hard to beat, but John had electrifying pace to go with it. The funny thing about him was that with all his fine attributes, John Reagan didn't have a girlfriend. Around the fair sex he was useless, a jibbering wreck, always tending to say daft things bordering on the stupid, egged on by brainless hulks who called themselves forwards. In particular, one James Durrant, a loud-mouthed git from somewhere north of Newcastle. He must have had some intelligence but he hardly ever showed any. He had played in the second team that day and was bragging about the skirmishes he'd got into, trying to impress the first teamers that were present.

Along with John Reagan, he was studying psychology otherwise known as the 'nutters'.

"Hi John, you Yorkshire pudding." He always thought that this was a funny way of greeting me but after the hundredth time it ceased to be funny to me but he always gave a loud laugh as he said it. "Hit any cows lately?" Another bellowing laugh.

"Hi Jim, you Geordie git." I retorted. Jim was a bully, both physically and verbally. There were two ways of dealing with him, the best being to ignore him because he hated it. On this occasion I went with 'fight fire with fire' and duly received a punch to the chest for my sins!

The reason for his aggression towards those of us from Yorkshire was unknown but he was a person to avoid. Sadly for Johnny Reagan this wasn't an option as they shared the same room! This fact also added to John's failure to find a girlfriend. Sharing and sleeping in the same room with someone like Durrant was the 'kiss of death' to any relationship!

It's terrible to say but the only satisfaction I derived from talking to Jim was that his complexion was worse than mine. Wasn't that sad!

We had just drunk our first pint and the drinking games were about to start when I was tapped on the shoulder. I turned round to find the girl that I had chosen earlier stood before me. Before Durrant had any chance to embarrass me or the young lady, I took hold of her hand and led her out of the bar.

The expected catcalls and whistles duly followed us. "The Yorkshire Pudding's got a bird." And worse.

"I'm sorry to bother you but I don't know what to do." She said rather apologetically.

"What's the problem?"

"None of my friends have been brought in. It's our first time trying to get into the disco."

"What do you want me to do?"

"Could you get one of your mates to go out and get Denise. She's my best friend."

"They'll have already brought somebody in and you can't sign in two people in one night. If you get caught trying to do that, they'll take your Union card off you."

"What can I do?"

"I'm not sure. Just wait there a minute and I'll check with the lads."

More ribald comments greeted my return to the bar. The games were well under way and the less mathematical players were well down their second pint.

I approached Johnny Reagan as he was the most likely person to not have signed someone in.

"Hey Johnny can I have a word?"

"We're in the middle of a game of 'names of', John."

"Yes, I know, but I want you to do someone a favour. Have you signed anyone in tonight?"

"No, why?"

"Good! Come with me. It'll only take a couple of minutes. Durrant will be on his third pint by then, the useless git!"

"OK. Sorry lads. Be back in a mo, boyos."

He followed me out to where the girl was standing.

"Hi. This is John. Johnny this is … Sorry I don't know your name!"

"It's Jeanette. Jeanette Smith."

"Well Jeanette Smith, this is John Reagan and he's here to help get your friend Denise into the dance, aren't you Johnny?"

"Will do, but how do I know which one she is?"

Jeanette replied with a very positive description. "She's dark-haired, slim, about my height and very pretty."

As he ran off to do his chivalrous best I shouted, "and she's called Denise!"

Whatever selection strategy Johnny used, he managed to select the correct girl and as Jeanette had said boy was she pretty! So pretty in fact I could tell she had a big effect on her 'knight in shining armour' Sir Johnny! How on earth she hadn't been selected before was an absolute mystery to me. Maybe, being her first time in the queue, her quiet disposition had not caught anyone's eye in the mass of girls that stood there.

The situation became a bit awkward as Denise and Johnny became very animated as they talked and laughed at the situation and poor Jeanette looked a little lost at what to do. I reasoned that my girlfriend Ann would understand the situation and the four of us left the rugby lot to their silly drunken games and entered the dance hall.

Fate proved to be a very positive influence for Johnny and Denise that day.

Eva

Joy was, as her name suggested a real joy; the type of friend everyone needs. Of course at the time, her enthusiasm and ultra-positive outlook on everything could be maddening but in general, she was such a lovely person to be around.

Since I had reluctantly agreed that she could come with me on my very dodgy quest to find John, she had become like a woman possessed. A woman literally on a mission.

She had researched everything about the late 1960s; the clothes, the news items, hairstyles, money, you name it and she had researched it on Google or in her dad's book. What she could not research was how we would get there. That was solely my department. She didn't have my powers of 'seeing' things and so it was left to me to do the 'travel plans'. Not that it was going to be as easy as going into a travel agents or booking on-line. My main avenues of researching travel arrangements were in hospitals where people had been born or had died. One might imagine graveyards would be a good place to meet ghosts and newly deceased people but this was a fallacy.

Rarely did people select a graveyard as their 'special place' to haunt. Contrary to public opinion, ghosts being present in graveyards is a myth since, if they didn't select it as their special place, they were highly unlikely to be born there and have you ever heard of someone dying in a graveyard?

I felt a little guilty about going into the hospital just to find a suitable ghost. It didn't seem quite right somehow as their main purpose was to keep people alive.

Strangely or not, a good source for this sort of quest was the local library. No, I don't mean that people die in libraries through some kind of boredom but there were many books about local sightings or hauntings in buildings in the area. There was absolutely no reason for me to think that I was the only person with my powers. In fact, in the 17th century I had met Mary when we were returning Valentine to his mother and she could do exactly the same things as I could do. I must admit it was a great relief to find out that I was not unique.

I had decided that I would catch the bus to the town's library and do some research on my own without the joy of Joy!

Whatever I found out was not going to be perfect. If I managed to locate the ghost of someone who was born in 1966 or 1967, the actual date, month and day, of their birth was where we would finish up and as in 1605 we had had no choice but to go back to Henry's date and place of birth.

The place of birth might present a few problems but unlike 1642 and 1605, the 1960s would provide reasonable transport links that didn't involve walking or travelling by horse and cart.

Joy's idea about backing that horse in the Grand National had real merit since the key date of birth was on or before 8th April 1967. I had done this sort of thing only once before and at that time had had the help of a very friendly man called Jon Stow who had just died on April 6th 1605 when I met him. He had put us in a situation to find a person who was about to be born in a very convenient place and time for us to complete our mission of returning Valentine to his mother.

Maybe that was the basis of the plan. After all, I did have my namesake Nanna Eva, John's grandmother, with whom all my adventures began. She died in my bedroom on 25th May 1963 and I still saw her there on a regular basis. A strange thing to say but she was my guardian angel as she had saved my life in 1642 when I was only 11.

The library did have a few suggestions. There was a witch called Mary Panel who had been seen a number of times on a hill just outside town and a few stories about a man who frequented the 'Three Bridges', close to the village of Fairburn and its Ings.

That evening at about 10.30 pm Nanna Eva did appear. It was almost as if she knew I needed her. Nobody else could see her, but after my two time travelling adventures my family were well aware of Nanna Eva's existence and my ability to 'see' her.

"How are you Nanna Eva?" Always seemed a strange question of someone who had died 50 years ago. A smile and a 'fine' was what I got in return.

"Nanna Eva, I have a favour to ask. It might be impossible or even silly but nevertheless you know me, always having ideas." Another smile from Nanna Eva. She was such a lovely lady. In the ten years I had known her she was my source of sensible advice even through my early teenage years, but I was a little anxious about telling her about my latest idea.

She listened carefully as I explained my thoughts and what Joy and I were planning. I sensed that she wasn't too keen on my ideas and as she said that I was 'playing with fire' and although she didn't say it 'messing with her grandson's life'. She told me not to use my powers for trivial personal reasons.

The conclusion of the conversation was that she would see what she could do to find a suitable person to aid us in our travels. How she communicated with others in the spirit world she never discussed with me but my experiences with Jon Stow suggested such communications existed.

I had arranged to see Joy the next day at her house to report back on my findings at the library.

She was her usual self; buoyant, excited and talkative!

"Flower power. That's what we need!"
"What?"
"Flower power. All the rage in 1967."
"What on earth is flower power?"

Joy showed me a picture in her dad's large book. "There! Lots of gigs in open fields with people with flowers in their hair!"

"She has next to nothing on. Is this how we have to dress?" I said pointing at the semi-naked girl in the photo.

"We can hardly go in today's clothes. Half of them haven't been invented yet!"

"I don't think invented is the right word."

"You know what I mean. We don't want to stand out as being weird."

I looked at the photo again.

"You mean she doesn't look weird to you? You'd have to pay me a lot of money to dress like that!"

"We might need a lot of money to dress like that!"

"Too true."

"It might be useful to us if you read this book with all the happenings from late 1966 onwards to April 1967. It might be helpful to know what happened or what is about to happen."

"We can't change anything though Joy. Eva has given me a talking to about doing our adventure just for the fun of it."

"I always find it difficult when you say Eva. You're the only Eva I have ever known."

"Suppose it can be a bit confusing, but she is a bit older than me by just over 110 years!"

"And she is dead!"

"Yes, sadly she is. According to John, she was a really lovely lady when she was alive."

"Has she said anything to help us find someone?"

"No, not yet. I only mentioned it to her yesterday."

"We really should make a list of things we need to take." Joy concluded.

"OK. Fire away," I replied, "and I'll make a list. Got a pen and some paper?"

It took us some time to come up with a complete list, but about an hour later Joy was satisfied that we had the finished article.

"Now for things we cannot take." She said with some authority. "Mobile phones, money from today, credit cards or any card for that matter, IPods and IPads. What else has been invented since 1967?"

"Microwaves?" I ventured.

"We won't be taking one of those!"

"I didn't mean that. It's just one of the things we cannot talk about like, Tony Blair and Maggie Thatcher."

"Who in their right mind would want to talk about them?"

"We need to find out what bands and singers were famous back then and not talk about Lady GaGa or Madonna."

"With the big boobies!"

"That's a point. What TV shows were on then?"

"Not a clue, but they didn't have all the channels we have today. My dad says that they only had about two or three."

"How boring it must have been back then!"

The Spring Term has sprung

The Spring Term, as it was called, had started in late January. Things were going well although I could have worked harder and maybe now was the time to put in some real effort. The rugby was going well and I had made the odd appearance for the first team when Johnny Reagan unfortunately was injured. It's difficult replacing someone as good as Johnny but I was the next best they had.

The cleaner for our rooms on A stairs was a lovely lady called Mrs Smith. She used words and phrases that I'd never heard before. Talking to me and the other lads, words like 'hinny, canny lad and pet' were common. She had a daughter called Jeanette who sometimes would help her out when she wasn't working. I estimated that she was probably seventeen years old and was the target of much of the amorous advances of those whose rooms were on A stairs. Geoff (of big bits in the sink fame) had asked Jeanette out in the first term. Being that bit older and more self-assured not to mention the suave public schoolboy demeanour, he had been successful in dating her, much to her parents' reluctance to sanction the match. It didn't matter really as

Waiting in Line

the liaison finished before the end of the first term. The differences in their backgrounds and ages was much to blame because in their own way they were both nice people and both friends of mine.

As with Geoff's birthday party, there were many other parties thrown by members of the rugby club as various birthdays were celebrated. Some were more of the 'couple type' and I plucked up courage to ask Jeanette out to one such party, risking the wrath of her parents. It was a purely platonic relationship but we enjoyed each other's company and unlike Geoff I was only a year or so older than her. I am not sure she really enjoyed the student-way of doing things and we often left parties earlier than some of my friends. She worked at Marks and Spencer in the city centre and although I liked her a lot, we felt it was better if we agreed to be friends only.

My new attitude to work and the rugby took up most of my time and of course there was the business of selecting girls from the line on the way to the bar, although now I couldn't really ignore Jeanette if she was there.

Geoff and I were still partners in the second fifteen when we didn't get the call for higher things and although we came from different backgrounds, we got on really well. He wasn't quite as full of arrogance as some of the public schoolboys who owned cars and even race horses. Some of them were heavily into betting and had the money to do it. We had a séance one night and the so called ghost that 'visited' us spelt out the name of 'What a Myth' when asked who would win the Hennessey Gold Cup. A lot of student money including some from student grants went on that horse but none of mine (a true Yorkshireman!) and it lost. That's what I like, a ghost with a sense of humour! We didn't have any more séances after that!

Being three years older than me, Geoff was more mature than the rest of the students in our year but he still had, at times, a boyish sense of fun.

One evening after dinner, dressed in full gown attire, we decided to visit the Student Union for a quiet drink. There was no queue of girls since it was a Wednesday and we had had the afternoon off as the rugby had been cancelled due to the hard frost that had prevailed for the last three days.

Our other task that evening was to give blood. From time to time a hospital unit used the downstairs dance floor as a mobile blood collecting service. This was to be my second session although Geoff had done many more. The makeshift beds were there and only a small queue of students waiting to do their bit. Although there were biscuits and tea for after, Geoff and I had eaten and were bar-bound for the aforementioned quiet drink.

Geoff went first and whilst he was being connected, I was called over to the adjacent bed.

"Lie down, head this end please," came the nurse's command. I am no good with ages but possibly she was in her mid-thirties. She had a pleasant disposition but there seemed to be a slight hint of tiredness in her voice.

Waiting in Line

"Thanks." I said dutifully and laid down the correct way. About halfway through my session, I noticed Geoff had finished and was recuperating.

"Hurry up John," he said, as if I could make the blood drip faster. Eventually, I had given 'an armful' as one comedian had said.

"Do you want tea and biscuits? They're over there." The nurse enquired.

"No, it's OK. We've just eaten. Is it OK if I get off? He's waiting." I said pointing to Geoff.

"You should really rest for a few minutes."

"I'll be OK." I insisted with a touch of 'machoism'.

Geoff and I walked out of the hall. "Last person to the bar buys the drinks."

Now the bar we were headed for was up two flights of stairs and he was already five yards ahead by the time he had issued the challenge. I followed in quick pursuit. Up the first flight of stairs, then the second. On reaching the top a strange feeling came over me. I decided to pretend to look at the notice board because I felt very dizzy and needed some support.

The next thing I knew Geoff was slapping my face as I lay on the floor. "You don't get out of paying for the beer that easily my friend!" So much for friendship!

The crowd that had gathered around thought this immensely amusing. I was not too sure.

Eva

Joy had been a real help with her research but suddenly, whether or not because of what Nanna Eva had said, I was beginning to have cold feet about the whole expedition.

Anyway there may be no such person to enable our transit back in time. If Nanna Eva was dead against my 'thoughts' and 'plans' she might sensibly not help in finding such a person.

I hadn't seen her for a few days (or nights) so I was beginning to think that I was right in my assumption that she didn't want to help. Suddenly, as if she could read my mind, she appeared as I laid listening to my Adele CD. I pulled the earpieces out not only to be polite but to be able to hear what she said. My dad said that I always had my music on far too loud, although how he knew I haven't the foggiest.

"Good evening Nanna Eva," I said as politely as I could. "Any news?"

She looked straight ahead at me with her grey-blue eyes which seemed to have a look of doubt in them as opposed to the usual smiling nature. She was always dressed the same in a long flowing white dress down to her ankles.

She moved closer.

"Eva, are you really sure that you want to go through with this. Your mercy missions with Valentine were your attempt to help someone who needed you. This latest journey is purely for your own pleasure and interest."

"Yes, I know. I am having doubts about the whole thing but I seem to have backed myself into a corner by telling Joy she can come too. She's very excited about the whole thing."

"Involving others seems only to make matters worse. Things can go wrong, Eva. Joy may not understand the consequences of what might happen. Remember Grace?"

Grace was the young policewoman who had unfortunately got involved in the return of young Valentine. Sadly, she had been scarred for life when gunpowder exploded at Coughton Court.

"Yes, I do. I feel really guilty every time I think about her, but as my mum says, everything we do in life comes with risks."

"You ought to explain to Joy what happened to Grace as a warning."

"Yes, I will Eva, although I doubt it will have any effect on her decision to go." In fact, I had already mentioned to Joy about what had happened to Grace, but it had not altered her desire to come with me.

I paused for a moment and then carried on. "You've found someone who can help us haven't you, Nanna Eva?

You wouldn't be so serious if there was no chance of us going, would you?"

"No, you are correct. I have found someone who is willing to help. It will mean that you have to travel to a town called Beverley."

"Where's that?"

"Not too far away. It's in Yorkshire but it is in East Yorkshire not West."

"Who is it?"

"The ghost of a young teenage girl called Alice. She was born on April 8th at 11.05am in Beverley and she died by falling out of a second floor window. The house she haunts is called Norwood House which is close to the centre of Beverley, so it shouldn't be hard to find. Be careful though, she can be a bit mischievous!"

WEIRD GIRLS AND STRANGE GOINGS ON

The queue of girls was longer on a Saturday than either Friday or Sunday and there was a direct correlation between the length of the queue and the fame of the pop group or singer that was on.

In truth, in the strictest sense of the word, it wasn't a queue. In a queue the first girl in the queue would be the first girl to be chosen to enter the dance hall. This wasn't the case. Sadly, the criteria that the male students used to select a girl wasn't on the basis of who had been standing there the longest. It would show the shallowness of the male selection process if I said how they were chosen.

The selection of girls waiting in line gave me a bit of an idea. Most of the rugby crowd didn't have girlfriends whether that was because they were of a 'type' that girls didn't fancy or whether they were too involved in their sport to be bothered with girls I wasn't sure. Some did have girlfriends who were miles away at home or at other educational establishments.

So I was in a good position to put the two together; the girls waiting in line and the relationshipless rugby players. It might in time be a sort of money spinning dating business, although I couldn't see too much of a future in that kind of thing.

I had heard through the grapevine that one of our star players Johnny Reagan had met a very pretty girl in the line and they were dating seriously now. My first focus of attention might be to get Jeanette Smith, our cleaner's daughter, a boyfriend to suit her lovely personality. She was, after all, pretty and nice but a little on the shy side. She hated the line she had to wait in each weekend.

The victim or partner I had selected for Jeanette was Andrew Massey. He passed the test on the good-looking stakes, with his dark hair and chiselled features. He was from Lewes in Sussex and we had had plenty in common and lots of time to talk about things on an away fixture to Carlisle the week before. His home town was only a few miles away from where my grandfather was born and I had had many a summer holiday playing on the South Downs and on the pebbly beach at Brighton.

The one thing we didn't have in common was that he spoke in a much more elegant and refined way than I did. Never once did I hear him say 'shut t' door' or 'off to t' town'. There might be a bit of a language barrier between him and Jeanette but the risk was, in my opinion, worth taking.

Surprisingly, Andrew was unattached and despite the language differences, he was, in my book, an ideal partner for Jeanette. As Saturday approached, I mentioned that after the match I was going to listen to the group that was on at Dunelm House. It was a group called the Tremeloes and they had just released their first single on their own called 'Here comes my baby' and it had risen to number four in the charts.

He agreed that he was doing nothing and fancied an after match pint once the opposition from Gosforth had departed. As we walked along the line that Saturday night, I chose Jeanette with Andrew in mind. Andrew, in turn chose a girl. She was quite tall about my height of five feet nine inches with unnaturally jet-black hair. She had a very round symmetrical face with piercing blue eyes and was by far the most elegantly dressed girl in the line. She had the most gorgeous smile and I could see why Andrew had chosen her.

Once we were inside I introduced Jeanette to Andrew and politely they shook hands. Andrew in turn introduced the tall girl to us as Jenny.

"What's your name?" She suddenly said to me in an accent I immediately recognised and it wasn't a Geordie one. "Are you called John?" For some reason, I felt quite threatened by this seemingly forward question.
"No, I'm Alan." I lied as I attempted to wink at Jeanette and Andrew for back-up.
"Where do you come from?" She continued her questioning.
I turned to Andrew and Jeanette. "Do you two want to go down to the dance hall whilst I talk to ... Sorry what was your name again?"
"Er ... Jenny." She stuttered seeming unsure of her name.

Jeanette and Andrew began to walk down the steps to the dance hall. I turned once more to face this strange girl. "Do you want to go down to the dance hall?"

"No thanks. I'm waiting for my mate. She's still outside. How do I get her in?"

"You can't really. She'll have to wait until someone picks her and signs her in."

"Can't you do it?"

"No, I've just signed Jeanette in and you can only sign in one person."

"That's stupid. Where do you come from?" There was that question again which once more made me slightly uncomfortable.

"Yorkshire." I said.

"Whereabouts?"

"Near Leeds." I said as vaguely as I could, not liking the third degree questioning.

"I'll wait here and see what happens to … er my mate, Hayley."

With that, I took the opportunity to depart down the stairs.

What a strange girl! There was definitely something not quite right about her, but I wasn't at all sure what it was. She was however very attractive despite her strangeness.

Eva

I walked to Joy's house to tell her the news.

"Eva says that she's found somebody who was born in early 1967 and who haunts a house in a town called Beverley."

"Where's that?"

"Over in East Yorkshire towards Brid."

"Never been there."

"Brid?"

"No stupid. That town called Beverley."

"Me neither. Oh, and while I remember, Eva says there's another thing we should do."

"What's that?"

"Change our names."

"Change our names?" Joy repeated.

"Yes, if we don't John might remember meeting me and that might change the future."

"I don't quite understand."

"Well, when John is sixtyish he meets me when I'm eleven-years-old."

"Come again?"

"This time thing is confusing but I've met John twice before when I was younger and he was older. If he meets an Eva when he is eighteen he might just remember me later when I'm eleven. No, you're right, it doesn't make much sense at all."

"I think I get it. Shall I change my name too? Just to be on the safe side. In case he meets me when I'm younger!"

"Suppose so, but what names shall we use?"

"I've often wanted to be called Beyoncé." Said Joy.

"Might be a bit too new a name. We need something that fits with 1967."

"Have you got a middle name?" Joy enquired.

"No. I'm just plain Eva Mills."

"I'm just plain Joy Black."

"You could change your name to Cilla. That would be 1960ish." I suggested.

"Ha! It's a bit too twee for me. I need something that matches my character!"

"You mean Jack Black?"

"Very funny. No, something that says I'm a party animal."

"Do what Cilla Black did and change to another colour. She started her life as White."

"Not a bad idea."

"How about Jenny Grey," I offered another sensible suggestion.

"I sound like a bird, but I like Grey. How about Marci Grey? We have a friend called Marci and I always liked her name."

"It's funny that. If you like someone then you often like their name."

"Suppose so, but is Marci a name for 1967?"

"Doubt it. Let's stick with Jennifer or Jenny for short."

"Jenny Grey it is. That's if I can remember it. Must practise with each other otherwise we might come unstuck."

"Yes, good idea. What about me?"

"Something that matches your cheeky personality, like …… Pinky Mills!"

"Ha! Thanks a bundle Jenny! I always wanted to be called Charlotte. At school, some boy nicknamed me Hayley because of some actress they had seen in an old film called Hayley Mills."

"Sounds nice, Hayley. The Mills part needs a bit of modification though."

"Can we be sisters, Jenny? Hayley Grey ….. sounds OK doesn't it?"

"Do we look like sisters?" Joy enquired.

"No, not really." I replied. "OK. Hayley Black is what I'll have. I might remember the Hayley Mills bit and your surname!"

"Isn't this exciting!" Joy was her usual effusive self.

"There is something that Eva says I must warn you about, Joy."

"This sounds serious."

"It is in a way."

Again, I explained about Grace and the accident that befell her and I tried my hardest to describe some of the difficulties that we might face.

"It's not like going back to the Civil War is it? The 1960s weren't that bad." She retorted.

"No, that's true. No Cavaliers or Roundheads!"

Lies, damned lies and statistics

The strange tall girl was once again in the line the following Friday. I tried to ignore her but she stepped out of the line right in front of me.

"Hi Alan. This is my friend Hayley. Will you sign her in?"

At first I wasn't sure that she was talking to me, then I remembered my lie. That's the problem with lies, you have to remember what you said!

"Oh hello, it's er …Jenny isn't it?" I just remembered in time.

She looked at me blank as did her friend Hayley who then turned towards Jenny and gave her a funny look. It seemed ever so odd but the town girls can be like that sometimes I thought, although they were not usually as forthright as these two.

"Oh yes, that's right, it's Jenny."

Waiting in Line

I saw Hayley give her another strange look. This pair seemed to be from another planet or maybe Lancashire, I thought!

"Yes, I don't mind signing her in but I have none of my friends with me to sign you in." I didn't really mind signing her in because I had another match to set up with a mate, Colin who was probably going to arrive at any minute.

"Not a problem. Hayley wants to ask you something, don't you Hayley?"

I ignored the last part of what she said as did her friend and walked with Hayley towards the Union building. I signed her in and as I turned to leave her waiting for the bossy Jennifer to be selected and signed in, another question duly arrived.

"Is your name John?" Hayley asked.

I looked at her quizzically. "What's all this about me being called John. Your mate Jenny asked me the same question last week." And I don't like being interrogated, I should have added. Did she know I was lying?

She looked embarrassed. "Sorry. You look a lot like a friend of mine called John."

"Well my name is Alan," I reconfirmed my lie.

"From Leeds?"

"Yes, from Leeds." I did not like the way this conversation was going. "Is there something the matter with me? Why are both of you interested in where I come from?"

"Sorry, no reason. It's just that we are looking for someone called John and he comes from Castleford."

I stared at her. There was something unreal about this conversation. "I'll ask around to see if I can find someone who fits the bill. There are a lot of Johns around. Why do you want to find him?"

"Oh, no reason really, except he is a cousin of mine."

"OK, I'll see what I can do," and with that I made my hasty exit down the stairs.

JOHN

Because of the 'cow incident' and the stupid hand injury that was still plaguing me after all this time, I couldn't play sport and so I was getting fat. I had had to go home and attend yet another appointment at Pontefract General Hospital over the Christmas break and it had been decided by the specialist in charge of such injuries that the bones in my hand had not set right and had to be re-broken and reset. Not something I was looking forward to as it involved a general anaesthetic.

Usually to go home to see my parents and Ann, my girlfriend, I hitched lifts down the A1. It was quite easy to do. Many people stopped to give me lifts; lorry drivers, fellow students richer than me who could afford a car and more elderly couples who were on a day trip out somewhere and wanted to help a poor student. Once I got a lift right from the 'Angel of the North' public house to where Ann was at college in Derbyshire. Usually however, hitching involved more than one lift and sometimes a bus ride as I got nearer home.

On this occasion, I decided to catch the train home. I stayed in hospital for one night after the re-breaking and felt well enough two days later to catch the train back to Durham.

It was as I was standing on the platform at York station that I first noticed the two girls. They were dressed in a strange way that was difficult to describe, probably in the latest gear from Oxford Street in London. They looked totally lost.

"Does the next train on this platform stop in Durham?" Said the taller of the two.
"Yes, it does. Are you new students?" I asked.
"Yes, that's right. Will it be a steam train?"

Strange question I thought. I had been a bit of a trainspotting anorak in my early teenage days but sadly there hadn't been any steam trains since about 1964.

"No, it will be a diesel train. Sadly, they're all diesel now. Steam trains were all scrapped some years ago. There are a few left but they are mostly in museums."
"I need the toilet," the smaller one said. "Is the train due soon?"
"No, you have a few minutes. The toilets are over there behind the kiosk."

They seemed to look at each other blankly, but then headed off in the direction that I was pointing.

I didn't see them again for some time. In fact, we had reached Darlington when suddenly they both appeared and seemed deliberately to sit in the seats opposite me, when in fact, there were many other free seats available. Another strange thing was that they had changed what they had been wearing!

"Can you help us?" Said the tall girl who seemed to be the more outgoing of the two. "We haven't been to Durham before and are not sure where to go."

"Didn't you have an interview in Durham last year when you applied?"

They looked at each other as if needing some kind of consensus of opinion.

The smaller one replied. "No, we got in without an interview."

This did seem strange but I had read somewhere that more girls were being encouraged to apply to universities and were at this time being offered places, maybe with lower A level grades, to offset the large numbers of males currently studying for degrees. With my poor A level record and yet still being accepted, I could not complain about this turn of events.

"Could we ask you a favour?" The tall one continued. "We have nowhere to stay in Durham. Do you know of anywhere?"

"Which college are you at? Surely they will provide rooms in halls of residence or in digs?"

Again they looked at each other as if searching for some combined answer.

"St Matildas," the taller one said.
"You mean St Marys?"

"Yes, that's the one. St Marys."

"They have a hall of residence for all fresher students, I think. You are a bit late arriving at the University, this is the second term of the year."

"We got delayed. We had problems. Do you know where we could stay?"

"Well, there should be someone at the Student Union building who can possibly point you in the right direction and there must be some estate agents with flats to let. Durham is quite a compact city so visiting the various estate agents shouldn't require too much walking around."

"Can you show us where this Student thingy building is?"

"Student Union. Yes, it's easy to find. From Palace Green where the Cathedral is situated, it's just down Bow Lane and across Dunelm bridge. I'll walk you there if you want."

"Thanks. That would be great."

"Did you back the Grand National winner yesterday?" A strange question from the tall girl.

"No, but I wish I had. I don't gamble but my granddad Tom does. He backed Rondetto, but I think it fell."

"We backed it!! Foinavon 100-1!"

"Wow, well done." I think I was impressed but a little uneasy that these two teenage girls gambled.

EVA

Joy and I practised calling ourselves Hayley and Jenny. My mother thought we had gone 'do lally'.

"It's just a joke mum." I said. "All the girls at school have been doing it."

"Sounds crazy to me. How do you know whether they are talking to you?" Mum asked.

"Well, I'm Hayley and Joy is Jenny for the week."

"Daft I call it. And what about those silly hairdos you've both got? You are not going back to school in September looking like that."

"We are not going back to school. Hopefully, university, mum."

"Oh yes, I'd forgotten."

Most of our plans had been put into operation. Appropriate clothes had been bought (from a charity shop), hair done the right way despite mum's disapproval (or so we thought) and a little money from Joy's granddad that he had saved from before decimalization. There were lots of different coins that he had found in various places in his house. He thought that he could maybe use the pennies in old 'one arm bandits' as he called them and the rest, he hoped might be worth a 'bob or two' in the future. We were destined to put all of it on a horse, a real certainty, in every sense of the word!

The big thing that Joy and I had to discuss was the 'lie' we were going to tell our parents. Most of our friends were going to take a year out before going to college or university, but we had both agreed that a year was too long. We thought a month in 1967 would be sufficient, so we had to have a cover plan for one month.

Joy hit upon the idea of working for the summer in a resort down on the south coast. Going to Ibiza or Magaluf for a month would be an unlikely story, even just from the point of view of the amount of money needed, not to mention the passport implications.

My dad was all in favour of me earning money throughout the summer months, although mum had her reservations about us being away for so long. The argument that when I went to university I would be away for a lot longer was a deciding factor in her coming round to our way of thinking.

So eventually mum agreed, but she needed to know who we would be working for and where we would be staying. Joy had the same difficulty with her parents or rather her mother. It's understandable that mums are more worried about their daughters leaving home for any length of time but teenagers must spread their wings and leave the nest.

We chose Brighton because Joy had been there with her family and they knew somebody who ran a B&B there. Joy's mum even went to the length of contacting them and buying a train ticket for the journey, there and back on a monthly return basis. Meanwhile, I bought two train tickets to Beverley via Hull!

As June turned into July and the weather warmed up a little, we packed our two large backpacks for the journey and our stay in Durham. We only decided to take essentials, although you wouldn't have believed it looking at Joy's bag. Joy's dad took us to Castleford railway station early on the Monday morning to catch the train to Doncaster and from there, theoretically, to London's King Cross station.

For some reason Joy had dyed her hair jet-black. "Thought it went well with the 'flower power' theme." She had said. We did have a piece of good fortune in that in order to get to Hull we had to change at Selby and the Selby train left after the Doncaster train had departed. We just had to convince Joy's dad that he needn't wait to see us onto the train. He didn't take too much persuading as he had to get to work.

We had to wait around for about an hour and a half. Joy was getting more excited by the minute.

"What happens when we get to Beverley?"
"I've written down some instructions that Eva gave me. We have to find Norwood House in Beverley which shouldn't be too far away from the station. We might need to ask for directions. It's near the Bus Station and Beverley High School apparently. Then we need to contact Alice."
"Who the heck is Alice?"

"Oh, I forgot to mention it. She's the ghost we're going to use to get back in time. She was born on April 8th 1967 so we can, with her permission travel back to then."

"Does she know we are coming?"

"That's one thing I don't know."

"How did she die?"

"Do you really want to know?"

"Is it gruesome?"

"Not really. She was a young girl who fell from a second floor window. The only other piece of information Eva gave me was that she was very mischievous."

"Maybe the reason why she fell out of the window. Explain this 'corridor of transit' thing to me again. I still don't quite understand."

For what must have been the fourth time I did my best to explain what happened from what I knew of it.

"As far as I know a spirit can haunt or rather be at one of three locations; their place of birth, their place of death and a special place, presumably selected by them. I have, it seems, the special power to see them and what's more in walking towards and through them I can descend what seems to be a long bright corridor. This corridor takes me to one of these three locations."

"Does the person go with us?"

I thought for a moment about what had happened before and yes, she was right, the person also comes with us to the destination of the 'corridor of transit'.

"Yes, they do. I'd never thought of that."

"And the corridor ends in the place they were born and in the year they were born?"

"Yes, but even more than that, at the precise moment that they were born which does mean we could finish in a different place than where we started and at a different time of day. Nanna Eva said that Alice was born on April 8th at 11.05 but she didn't mention the exact place except that it was in the local maternity hospital."

"You've forgotten something we have to do when we get to Beverley." She said, a mischievous smile on her face. "We have to put all our money on Foinavon at the bookies!"

"Don't be daft. There is no way any bookie will take a bet on a horse that won a race nearly thirty years ago!"

She looked blank and slightly crestfallen at my rebuke.

"Let me explain again, you dipstick. When we get back to Beverley on April 8th in 1967 then we can put all our money on Foinavon, because at that time the race hasn't been run and as yet our favourite horse hasn't won."

"You are right Eva, I am a dipstick but I did do some research on how we might raise more money. You never know how much we might need, so I thought it would be important." Joy explained.

"What kind of research?"

"Well, things like 'who won the Rugby League Cup in May 1967?' and the same thing for the football and other races such as the Derby. Here I made a list."

Sure enough, there was almost an encyclopaedia of dates and winners of various events from the sixties, seventies, eighties and nineties.

"Why do we need all those facts; we are not staying that long?"

Joy seemed to blush a little. "I just got a bit carried away. We'd better not use the same bookies in Durham though, they might get slightly suspicious."

"You have been doing some thinking. Well done Jenny!" And with that the train arrived.

RETURNING A FAVOUR

I was beginning to worry about the lies I was telling Jenny and Hayley and feeling guilty, but their persistent questioning was worrying me. So much so that I avoided the 'line' the following week. We had been playing away in Newcastle so I decided to stay up there until late with the rest of the team.

Andy seemed to have hit it off with Jeanette so I didn't need to worry about taking her in to the Student Union anymore. I did begin to look through the team and my college mates to see if there were two likely suspects that I could introduce to Jenny and Hayley, even if it was just to get them off my back.

Geoff 'big bits in the sink' Wainwright owed me a big favour.

"Look, all I want you to do is to pretend to be called John and say that you come from Castleford in Yorkshire."
"What with my accent!"
"Practise a few 'shut t' doors' or say that you were born in London and came up north to Yorkshire as a teenager and that accounts for your posh London accent."

"Have I really got a posh London accent?"

"You must be kidding me. It's like talking to someone who's got a 'gobstopper' in his mouth."

"What's a 'gobstopper'?"

"My point exactly! Look, it's only for one night while we get to the bottom of why they are pretending to be cousins of mine and wanting to find me."

"It seems strange, I must admit. They came from out of the blue didn't they?"

"No, they came from waiting in line!"

"What?"

"Never mind. Will you do it for me? Yes or no?"

"I suppose I ought to, given what you did for me on my twenty-first birthday bash."

"Yes, exactly and oh by the way, you are only eighteen and I've never had a birthday bash in all my life!"

That Saturday night in late April was the night of the last match in the season. Rugby wasn't played in May by order of the Rugby Football Union.

As Geoff and I approached Dunhelm House, I could see Jenny and Hayley waiting in the line. Jenny was one of the taller girls and with her jet-black hair was easily recognisable. Hayley was smaller with lighter coloured hair that looked more natural.

I took the proverbial bull by the horns.

"Hi Jenny, hi Hayley. This is John from Castleford. I said that I'd find him. These are your cousins John." I turned to Geoff.

He looked uncomfortable but I had removed the big bits from the sink and that felt a lot worse than uncomfortable!

"Hi," he said and with that Hayley grabbed his arm and marched him off towards the door.

"Shall we go Jenny?" Her eyes, not for the first time, seemed to go blank and then she recovered herself. "Oh yes, let's go."

When we were inside, Geoff and Hayley were deep in conversation and I wasn't too bothered about finding out what they were talking about. Hayley was all over Geoff who must have thought all his Christmases had come at once.

"Shall we go down to the dance, Alan?"

I still hadn't got used to my lying change of name.

"Alan," she repeated, "you seem miles away."
"Yes, OK, sorry. Let's go!" And with that she grabbed my hand and we set off down the first of four flights of steps to the dance hall.

It didn't feel too uncomfortable holding hands with Jenny. She did have lovely blue eyes and that jet-black hair made her really stand out but she did seem a little less extrovert than she had first appeared.

"What band is on tonight?" Joy asked.
"Band? Oh, you mean group. It's Manfred Mann. They've just released their latest record, 'Ha ha said the clown'. It's at number four."

"I know all about them." Joy said with a degree of pride. "They had a number one hit with 'Do wah diddy diddy' and 'Pretty flamingo'", and she burst into song as we descended the final set of stairs into the dance hall.

JOY

We arrived in Hull and caught the train to Beverley. Eva hadn't said too much more about Alice and where we would meet her but I trusted her as she seemed to know what she was doing.

I had no idea what Beverley was like. I had never been there before. We left the station and Eva said that we had to find Wednesday Market. She asked a woman for directions and we were not too far away. Within minutes we were in Wednesday Market.

"We need Toll Gavel now." Eva said.
"That's a funny name for a street." "She said that it's over there, down Butchers' Row."
I smiled. "The person who named these streets had a sense of humour!"
"Maybe they were the 'cool' names to have when they were named."
"What? Butchers in a boat, rowing down a street with a judge's hammer and asking for money?"
"Now you put it like that, maybe not!" Eva laughed.

Beverley seemed a very pretty town with lots of people around. I guess some were tourists because I'd heard that Beverley had a lovely church called a Minster for some reason, not a Cathedral I guess because Beverley wasn't a city, just a town.

As it was Monday there was no market in Wednesday Market. We walked past Boyes, Marks and Spencer and several charity shops and cafes. We came to a fork in the street and the right hand one declared itself to be Walkergate.

"This isn't the quickest way to Norwood House but I'm looking for the bookies and hoping it was there in 1967. We might not have much time to place our bet. Norwood House is down there," she said pointing down Walkergate, "but let's go left and see if we can find the bookies."

She stopped an oldish-looking man and I was too far away to hear exactly what she said but the look of surprise on his face was clear for me to see. She walked back to where I was standing.

"It's down here towards Saturday Market. I don't think that man took kindly to a teenage girl asking him where the bookies was!"

"That's why he looked surprised."

We passed more charity shops and two W H Smiths and ahead we could see a bandstand.

"There it is. William Hill, bless him. You are going to lose a lot of money you are my old son!" Eva said with a big smile on her face.

"Which way to the ghost?" I had to admit that I was getting a little nervous about what was to happen. I can safely say that I had only ever seen one ghost before and that was Nanna Eva and even then I was a little on the drunken side. Now, being stone cold sober it was with a real mixture of excitement and trepidation that I followed Eva across Saturday Market.

THE MYSTERY DEEPENS

Jenny asked me if I wanted to dance. I had decided that I had to keep Jenny away from Hayley whilst Geoff (or was it John) was getting to the bottom of the mystery.

At first there were just disco dances. Occasionally, I caught sight of Jenny looking at me with those beautiful blue eyes and thought that maybe my initial diagnosis of her being some sort of crazed demented woman was wrong. I smiled back as I attempted my best pathetic moves. I enjoyed dancing but didn't feel that I was particularly good at it. However, there was no doubt that Jenny was a good mover, doing things that I'd never seen on a dance floor before.

She was dancing so sexily that she was getting a lot of admiring looks from the lads around. I felt quite proud that Jenny was with me and at the same time a bit jealous of all the other lads looking at her. These were two emotions that I had never really experienced before.

Eventually we sat down. "I really enjoyed that," she said, "but the music is a bit different to what I'm used to."

"You are a very good dancer. How do you mean, the music is different to what you are used to? Manfred Mann and the other groups are playing all the latest pop songs from this year."

"It's not exactly garage or grunge is it?"

"Not what?"

"Oh, I mean … never mind. The hall is packed. I wonder where Eva and John are?"

"Eva?"

"Sorry Hayley. Getting mixed up. It's all this dancing. It's warm in here isn't it?"

Then a really strange occurrence happened. A lad called Jim Durrant asked Jenny to dance. He was one of the few rugby players that I wasn't that keen on. His Geordie accent rang out above the music.

"Haway, you dancin' lass?"

Whether Jenny had sensed something or not I don't know.

"Get stuffed spotty." She said with a great deal of aggression.

Durrant was not one to be denied. He pushed me hard in the chest in order to gain some of his macho pride back and to get to Jenny.

Jenny's slap to Durrant's head was only marginally faster than her knee to his groin. He sunk to his knees clutching his obviously painful region.

"Do that again and I'll put you in hospital and in the courts for assault."

I was so gobsmacked that I cannot remember Jim's reply. Let's just say he walked away with his tail between his legs to the applause of all those around.

Jenny was not a girl to be messed with.

"Sorry about that, Alan. He shouldn't go throwing his weight around. Men like that do annoy me. Again I'm ever so sorry."

"Don't let it worry you. You seem to have made everybody's day and Jim won't be able to live that down for some time!"

We enjoyed a few more dances and once again Jenny was the centre of attention. We didn't see Hayley and Geoff until the end of the evening. I had really enjoyed my time with Jenny. She had been great company and how she dealt with Jim had made my night. Her sense of fun and vitality, and most of all the sexy way she danced was amazing. Yes, she did say some silly things that I didn't understand, but I put that down to the nerves of being in my company!

The one thing that did stick in my mind was her jet-black hair and the way it was matched by the way her eyebrows had been enhanced with some kind of thick black pen. The way she was dressed wasn't quite the usual 'townie' girl look, but I'd come to the conclusion that she was the girl for me so long as I learned to duck when she used her right hook!

I wasn't usually one for compliments but I found myself saying. "Your hair is a beautiful colour and I do like your eyebrows. Where does your hair colouring come from?"

I expected the reply 'my mother has dark hair. I expect I must get it from her'. What I didn't expect was the answer she gave me which was: "It's from a bottle. L'Oréal, I think. I did it last week before we came here. I had the slugs done at the same time."

I let the slugs pass. "Where did you come from? Do you have a job?"

Jenny seemed to pause for a moment, clearly thinking about her answer.

"We got a train from York and Hayley and I are having a bit of a holiday before we go to uni."

"Which university?"

"Depends on my results. They come out in August. I did OK in the exams so I'll have to wait and see."

"But you cannot have taken your A Levels yet, it's only April. Exams aren't until May and June."

She smiled and looked slightly worried as if she had said something that she shouldn't have.

"Sorry. I took my exams last year and then Hayley and I took a year out to travel and work before uni."

"You know your results already then, so why the indecision about where you are going?"

A moment passed and she said. "I am having to retake one exam this year to get enough points."

"Points?"

"I wonder where Hayley and John have got to? I can't see them on the dance floor."

She seemed a little upset, so I let the matter drop. We met up with Hayley and Geoff outside at the end of the dance. They appeared to be in quite a close clinch as if they had just parted from a lingering kiss.

Whether Jenny had come to the same conclusion or not, she made a lunge for my lips and before I knew it we were in a passionate embrace. It was very pleasant. Her lips were very soft and the kiss had something I had never experienced before ..... a tongue!

I really believe that I was taken aback by the passion in the kiss. It brought tears to my eyes. As we parted, all I could see was Jenny's smiling face. I turned towards Geoff and he had an inane grin on his face and I felt that I had gone red with embarrassment.

On the way back to our rooms after leaving the girls, Geoff was full of it. "She is such a lovely girl and you seemed to have 'pulled'. She does seem to have some strange ideas though. Anyway thanks John my boy for organising a lovely night out."

"You're welcome, but I'm a bit peeved that I get your regurgitated bits out of a sink and you get a great night out!"
"You appeared to be having a good time too."
"True. Are you seeing her again?"
"Oh yes, on Monday night. We are going for a Chinese meal." Geoff replied.
"There still is a bit of a mystery concerning those two though. Even if Jenny is the most beautiful girl I've ever dated and a very nice person, there's still something not quite right about her, although I can't for the life of me think what it is. She's real fun to be with and I like her a lot, but there's just something."

EVA

We walked across Saturday Market and through a narrow passage and then a courtyard towards the bus station. Eventually, we stood before Norwood House. It had fourteen windows, fifteen if you counted the round one on what looked like the second floor. Could that be the one Alice fell from to her death?

There was a small parking area in front of the house with a pointed metal fence and a gate wide enough for a car to enter on the left.

Joy looked nervous and to be fair so was I. I had never had to look for a ghost before. The spirits I had needed at other times had been there in front of me and, in the main, I had been attempting to help them in some way. Finding the ghost of a mischievous young girl worried me somewhat as things might not be as simple as I had envisaged.

"What are we going to do Eva?"
"I'm not sure, Joy. In an ideal world we should knock on the door, ask where the ghost has been most seen, find her and walk hand in hand into 1967."

"Sounds simple when put like that. When are we going to change into our 1960s clothes?"

"We could do it now or when we get into 1967. Probably best to leave it until later. Changing now might add to our difficulties. OK, here goes."

We opened the gate and walked down the short drive. I knocked on the door. There was no answer.

"Maybe they're at work."

"Probably. What shall we do now?"

"I suppose we just hang around here until someone comes. Let's have a look around the back of the house."

"Are you sure Eva?"

"You stay here and I'll go see what I can find."

Fortunately, the passage to the back of the house was secluded so no-one could see me. I looked in the nearest window. As we had assumed, the house looked empty. I walked backwards to look at the upstairs windows and something caught my eye. There was a young girl looking out of the window. I waved at her and she disappeared.

I returned to Joy to explain what I had seen. We needed to get into the house, either legally or illegally.

"I'd prefer to wait here for the owners and ask them if we can talk to Alice."

"How on earth is that going to happen? They'll think that we're mad and call the police."

"Joy, I have done this before and you will just have to trust me. The worst time was with a lady called Anne Stow. To show her that I had special powers I had to show

Anne her dead husband who had only just died. That wasn't pleasant."

"I shouldn't imagine it was."

We stood there for about two hours before someone arrived. We waited whilst the lady entered the house, then knocked on the door again. It was a few minutes before the door was answered. The lady was probably in her fifties and had a pleasant demeanour given that two strangers had just knocked on her door. I had practised roughly what I was going to say.

"I am sorry to bother you but we are doing a school project about certain aspects of Beverley. Would you mind answering a few questions? It won't take long. We are at the High School, in the sixth form, and we are doing a study of the paranormal. Have you had any occurrences of anything that might be unexplained?"

She smiled. "You've heard about Alice?"

"No, we haven't I'm afraid. Who is Alice?"

"Well, it is difficult to believe but it started about a month after we moved in. Things started to go missing. At first we thought it was the children playing games but when they eventually left home to go to college, things still went missing. The funny thing is that the missing items turn up again in other places. Take last Sunday, I put my glasses down whilst I watched the TV, went to the kitchen to make a cup of tea and when I got back they were nowhere to be seen. On Tuesday I found them in the bathroom!"

"So who is Alice? The ghost who steals things."

"You believe that sort of thing? Before we moved in here there had been rumours of Alice who was a little girl who fell out of the upstairs window to her death. We did some research and sure enough there had been such a death. It didn't put us off buying the house as we didn't believe in such things but over the years my husband and I have changed our opinions. It does scare us a little, but few people really believe us and maybe think we are a little crazy and eccentric."

I decided to come clean and see how she reacted to what might seem to her to be outlandish statements. "I know what you mean and what I am going to say to you now might worry you, but I have special powers that let me see spirits and if you want, and only if you want, I can get you to see Alice and even talk to her."

There was a stunned silence.

"You believe in Alice?"
"Yes, I've seen her. She was at the window, but disappeared when I waved at her."
"Which window?"
"Sorry, but I went around the back of the house. It was the one in the middle."
"The one she is thought to have fallen out of, you mean?"
"Is it? It's up to you. I know that it's hard to believe. For the first few years nobody believed me but now I can prove it. If Joy stays here and you lock her out, would it be possible for you and me to find Alice. Oh, by the way, I am Eva Mills and this is Joy Black."
"I'm Elizabeth, Elizabeth Henderson. I teach science at the High School. I cannot recall seeing you two at the school."
"It's a big school." I took a guess.

"Yes, and you are in the sixth form. I teach mainly years ten and eleven."

"You stay here Joy. I'll be back once we've met Alice."

This seemed to convince Elizabeth that it was a calculated risk worth taking. I am not sure I would have agreed if the roles had been reversed.

We climbed the ornate stairs to the first floor. "It's that bedroom over there."

"OK, let's go meet Alice." I was desperately hoping I hadn't scared Alice off by waving to her. Some of the ghosts I had met before liked to remain unseen and were shocked when I spoke to them. I was in luck though; as I stepped into the room I could see her by the window."

"Hello, Alice."

No answer. My experiences had shown me that some ghosts did become elective mutes either through shock or disbelief that anyone could see them.

"My name is Eva."
"She said that you would come and talk to me."
"Did she? I thought she might. Can I get Elizabeth to see you? It would help with you living together. You can still do your bits of mischief and I'm sure the family will enjoy it more knowing what you look like."

She did have bruising to the side of her face as a result of her fall but in general she looked like any young girl.

"I suppose so." Came her slightly truculent reply.

Waiting in Line

I beckoned Elizabeth towards me and put my hand on her shoulder, which I knew would bring Alice into view. There was a sharp intake of breath as Elizabeth saw her tormentor for the first time.

"Alice, this is Elizabeth. Elizabeth, this is Alice."
Elizabeth spoke first. "It's nice to meet you Alice. Thanks for all the fun you have given us hiding things."

Alice smiled.

"Eva said that you wanted to use my 'corridor of transit'."
"Yes please."
"What does she mean?" Enquired Elizabeth.
"I'll try and explain later."
I turned back to Alice. "Yes, Joy and I would like to do that. Is it OK with you?"
"Yes, it will be fun."
"No funny tricks though Alice, Eva wouldn't be pleased."
"OK." Alice replied still with a mischievous smile.
"With Elizabeth's permission I'm going to get Joy and then we can leave." I turned to Elizabeth. "Now you've seen Alice you can be a little less worried when things go missing. It will be like a game of hide and seek!"

At this point I removed my hand from Elizabeth's shoulder and for her, Alice disappeared.

"Where has she gone?" Elizabeth asked.
"Nowhere. She's still here but without my powers you cannot see her."
"Are you and Joy going somewhere?"

"Yes. I promise that I will come back and explain in more detail and let you have longer with Alice."

I knew that I had to come back here as this was the only route back from 1967. It would take Elizabeth completely by surprise as Joy and I would just suddenly appear, but that was for another day.

"My husband is not going to believe me."

"He will when I come back and show him!" With that we walked back downstairs to get Joy.

The following events were so familiar to me but for Joy and Elizabeth they were a shock and a complete mystery. As Joy and I, holding hands, walked towards Alice, the brightly lit corridor appeared. Joy suddenly went tense. From poor Elizabeth's point of view, Joy and I had just done a complete disappearing act.

JOY

"What are you doing here?" The women screamed at us. There were several people around what looked like a hospital bed. All of them seemed anxious that we were there except the woman in the bed who seemed oblivious to our presence. Suddenly there was a loud cry of a baby and everybody's attention turned away from us.

"Let's go." Eva said as she grabbed my arm and pulled me towards the door.

"Get out of here!" The women screamed again.

Once outside the door we found ourselves in a long corridor with lots of glass windows. Eva pulled me up the corridor towards a distant door which opened out into the fresh air.

It was a bright sunny day without a cloud in the sky.

"Come on Joy, we need to find the way out and back into Beverley."

"Where are we?" I said breathlessly, as we had been running away from something or somebody but I didn't quite understand what or who.

"That sign over there says we are in Beverley Westwood Hospital."

"Do you know the way out?"

"No, but there must be a sign for the exit somewhere around. Is anyone following us?" She puffed.

"Don't think so. Why should there be?" I was unsure what we had done wrong for anyone to want to chase us.

"I'll explain later. There's a sign over there and it points to the exit on the left, under that archway."

"Can we slow down?"

We had been running up to this point and with all the stuff in my backpack I was beginning to tire.

"OK, I think we're out of danger now."

"Danger?" I repeated. "What danger were we in?"

"How about being at the birth of a little girl, unannounced; bringing germs and whatever else as uninvited guests at the birth of someone we are not related to; trespassing on hospital property. Would you like me to continue?"

"No, I get the drift."

We were soon in the centre of Beverley by the bandstand and I was surprised to see that there seemed to be a market on which hadn't been there earlier.

"Now where was that William Hill betting shop?" Eva asked.

"Things look different from when we were here earlier and I don't just mean the market."

Eva smiled. It was one of those smiles that she usually gave me when she thought I was being a bit thick.

"What? What have I said?" I asked her, knowing the kind of reply I was going to get.

Waiting in Line

"You can be a bit thick sometimes, Joy!"

At least being able to predict what a friend is going to say is comforting even if what she says is an insult to my intelligence.

"What?" I repeated.

"This is 1967! There's a Woolworths shop over there. Did you happen to see it earlier? No, I don't think so, they went bust, remember? And there will be other differences too, such as no McDonalds!"

"No McDonalds. What did they eat?"

"Proper healthy food?"

"OK, less of the chat." Said Eva. "We need to place the bet on Foinavon, find somewhere to stay for the night after we've collected our winnings and then get train tickets to Durham." This was the Eva you didn't mess with. I hadn't seen her in this 'matter of fact' mood too many times before but enough to know you did what she said.

"What time is it?" She asked.

"My watch says 2.35pm."

"Yes, but that's wrong. It's a lot earlier than that. Nanna Eva said that Alice was born just after eleven, 11.05 if I remember correctly, so it must be getting on for midday now."

"I don't understand, Eva." I complained. Eva looked at me again. "Yes, I know, thick or what?"

"The corridor of transit brought us to the exact time and date of Alice's birth. Just after 11am on Saturday 8th April."

"Was Alice still with us?"

Eva smiled yet again. "Yes, there were two Alices in that room. One was dead and the other had just been born!"

There are times when saying nothing was the best option and this was one of those times.

We nervously entered the bookies. The clock on the wall said just after ten minutes past twelve o'clock. We got some funny looks from the men that were there in their natural habitat and it wasn't surprising that we were the only females in the room.

A man standing behind a glass screen called out to us. "Can I help you?"

I had been given the task of placing the bet because, according to my friend, I was the most forward of us two and, in Eva's opinion, I looked the oldest.

"Sorry, I've never done this before, but I would like to put a bet on for today's Grand National."

"Are you eighteen?"

"Yes and so is my friend." Why I added that I don't know.

"OK. I'll help you fill in the betting slip as it's your first time. What horse do you want to bet on and how much?"

This, I had practised! "I want to put £4-15-7d on Foinavon to win the Grand National."

You could hear the laughter and sniggers from all the men in the room.

"You might as well give the money to charity or me." One said.

"She is giving it to charity. Fred's charity!" They all laughed again.

"Are you sure you want to back Foinavon? It's a bit of a donkey. Honey End is the favourite, that might be a better bet or Rutherfords or Red Alligator. All three are good horses." Fred was trying to be helpful.

"No, we like the name Foinavon." I was really looking forward to collecting our winnings in front of all these men later in the day!

"OK, £4-15-7d on Foinavon to win the Grand National at 100-1."

I took my plastic bag which contained all the coins that my granddad had given me and emptied it onto the counter. The coins were a real variety and granddad had called them pennies, half-crowns, sixpences, shillings and 'threpny-bits'. I loved the way he said 'threpny-bit'. It was a small, brown coin and it had straight edges a bit like a fifty pence coin.

"Bin saving up 'ave we?"

I ignored the sarcasm. "How much do we get when it … I mean if it wins?" I was getting excited.

"Let me see. If it wins you get ……" He started to work it out on a piece of paper.

"Do you want to borrow my calculator?" Eva dug me in the ribs and it hurt.

"What?"

"Never mind."

"That will be four hundred and seventy-seven pounds, eighteen shillings and four pence. Oh, plus your stake money back so that's another four pounds fifteen and seven pence, making a total of four hundred and eighty-two pounds, thirteen and eleven pence! Here's your betting slip that you'll need to collect your winnings." He laughed as did all the men in the room.

We left with beaming smiles on both our faces. Information means money!

The Grand National race was due off at 4.15pm so we had some time to kill. Sadly, we had no money to buy any food or drink but we had had the foresight to bring some fruit and a bottle of water, both of which Eva assured me would survive the time travel.

We sat on the steps of the bandstand eating our fruit. The market was quite busy and I could hear the call of some of the stall holders as they tried to sell their wares. The shop fronts seemed different with less in the way of advertisements and there didn't seem to be as many cars around. Suddenly, a strange looking blue bus caught my eye. It was strange because it had a dome shaped roof! As I watched it go down the street it became clear why its roof was shaped that way. I could see at the end of the street that there was a sort of archway the bus had to pass under and the shape of the roof of the bus matched the archway perfectly in shape. How quaint!

I watched as people passed. There were quite a few miniskirts and the men seemed to have longer hair than I had seen before. I supposed that like the bookies there would be no computers or CCTV in the shops and everybody paid in pounds, shillings and pence. A van passed by with lots of bottles of milk making a clanking sound as it went over the cobbles and I saw a single policeman with a strange shaped hat similar to the dome shape of the bus. I had to smile. What a really quaint world 1967 was! Quite different to anything I had experienced before.

Waiting in Line

We decided to try and find a shop which sold televisions, since there was a good chance that the Grand National would be on. This was surprisingly easy to do, as across the street from the bandstand, a shop announced itself as Briggs and Powell with a large sign above its front window. In this window there were a number of televisions for sale and sure enough one of them had on the scenes from the Grand National at Aintree. The weather didn't look quite as good as in Beverley, but as the forty-four horses lined up at the start, I had butterflies in my stomach.

As the horses started the race, jumping and sometimes falling, there was no mention of Foinavon. Both the horses that Fred had mentioned, Honey End and Rutherfords were well to the fore. The carnage duly arrived at the 23rd fence and the only horse to clear it first time was, of course, Foinavon, the donkey from the back of the field that had absolutely no chance of winning.

Even with a massive lead, poor Foinavon was slowing drastically as it approached the last fence. Honey End's jockey had had time to remount, circle back and clear the fence despite loose horses and the mayhem and was now closing fast on our horse. Had I not known the outcome I would have bet that Foinavon would be beaten in the home straight, but as history shows it clung on grimly to win by a reasonable distance. The people around us were shocked but Eva and I were shrieking with laughter, even though we had known what was about to happen.

"Here we come Fred to get our four hundred and eighty-two pounds."

"Don't forget the thirteen shillings and eleven pence!"

"I won't. I hope that all those men who laughed at us earlier are there!"

Sadly, they weren't and Fred was not quite as jovial as he had been previously.

"Well done girls. Beginners luck!"

"You must have made a lot of money from those suckers who took your advice on which horses to back." I said mischievously. He gave us a lame sort of grin as we left with our small fortune.

"We need a Travel Lodge or a Premier Inn to stay in for the night before we catch the train tomorrow."

"You're at it again, Joy. This is 1967, There are no Travel Lodges or Premier Inns. There's a B&B I noticed near the station. We could try there."

This we did and stayed one night at a B&B run by a young man called Martin Potts, not too far from the station where next morning we bought our tickets to Durham. We travelled to York via Hull and Selby and arrived in plenty of time for our northern bound train. York is a big station and finding the correct platform for our train proved more difficult than we imagined. However, with the help of a student who was returning from a weekend at home, we found the toilets in order to change into our 1960s outfits and managed to get on the correct train!

We never did find out the student's name although he was easily identifiable by the pot on his right hand, presumably to fix a broken arm. However, he was very helpful in directing us to where we could get digs in Durham and, after a couple of nights in yet another B&B, we were able to rent a small house on Hallgarth Street for the princely

Waiting in Line

sum of three pounds and fifteen shillings a week. It was not too far away from Dunelm House, the Student Union building. Eva and I had discussed our 'find John' strategy and it included meeting students in the Student Union bar. Not too onerous a task!

So on Friday 14th April we arrived at the building to find a queue of girls outside the door. "Can't we go in?" I asked a blond girl at the end of the queue.

"Not until you get picked, pet." She replied.

"Get picked?"

"Yes, you can only get into the dance if a student signs you in. You have to wait here to be chosen."

Eva and I looked at each other in amazement. "We have to wait here until some boy picks us to go in?"

"That's about the sum of it, pet."

So there we were, stood in a line of girls waiting for a boy called John. Neither Eva nor I had the slightest clue of what John looked like, but we were trusting in fate. Fate didn't reply. We failed. Nobody selected us and after two hours we trudged home defeated.

"I thought that I might be able to recognize John by his eyes. Everything else can change but eyes never do and that's how I hoped to recognise him."

The following night after about an hour waiting in a far larger queue, because apparently a band called the Tremeloes was on, I decided to do something about it.

Two nice looking boys of about our age were walking across the bridge. The smaller one went for a pretty girl standing next to me, so I grabbed his mate by the arm and introduced myself as Joy!

I was in a bit of a tizzy once I realized that I had used the wrong name but I think I took him so much by surprise that he didn't hear me properly. He said that he was called Andrew and I pulled him towards the door. Once we were inside, I introduced myself to the smaller one as Jenny this time and asked his name. Sadly, he wasn't a John either, he was called Alan. I did notice that he winked at Andrew as he told me his name. He said that he was from Leeds. Suddenly Andrew took off with the pretty girl, she never said what her name was, and I was left with Alan. I didn't mind too much as I wanted to wait for Eva to get selected and join me. He said that he couldn't help as he had already signed the other girl in and he was only allowed to sign one person in per evening. We chatted for a bit and then he left in the same direction as the other two.

Eva never got selected and she was bitterly disappointed. So I decided to leave the building and join her.

"Nobody picked me. I feel like an ugly duckling."

"You're not ugly, it's just that there are so many girls to choose from. Anyway neither of those two boys was called John, although Alan does come from Leeds."

"Let's go home. I'm cold," and with that we left for Hallgarth Street and a reasonably warm room.

"We'll probably never find him." Eva said despondently as we got home.

"Yes, we will. Don't be so pessimistic. We've only been here a week."

A Chinese foursome

I saw Geoff the next day at breakfast. "When did you say you were meeting Hayley?"

"Tomorrow night. It is Monday tomorrow isn't it?"

"Yes, it is. Do you know where the girls are staying?"

"Hallgarth Street. Why?"

"You still owe me a big favour and so if you don't mind I'd like to see Jenny again, maybe have a foursome."

"Are you trying to cramp my style, John? I thought you said that Jenny was a crazy woman?"

"I maybe got that wrong. First impressions are not my forte."

Geoff smiled and said nothing.

"Did she give you a telephone number to contact her?"

"No. She said something about having a mobile phone, whatever that is, but there is no phone where they are staying. She does say some crazy things though. She told me that we'd had a female Prime Minister called Margaret something or other. I told her that Barbara Castle was the closest we'd got to one and she went bright red. She seems a little forgetful and dizzy at times but otherwise she's so sweet and lovely."

"Yes, Jenny has memory problems too. Must be hormonal."

"I wouldn't let them hear you say that. They do have something of an edge when it comes to comparing what they can do compared with men. Hayley was really upset about having to wait in a line for some male to select her. She says that it was demeaning to women and she's right, it is. They are both off to university this year. She calls it uni, which is strange, but they are waiting for their results."

"That's what Jenny was confused about too. How can they be waiting for results when they haven't taken their exams yet?"

"Hadn't thought of that. I'll ask Hayley when I see her."

"Tell you what I'll do. I'll come with you on Monday but not stay, just ask Hayley to pass on a message to Jenny to see if I can meet her sometime this week."

"OK."

"How is the 'pretending to be me' going down?"

"She seems so pleased that I am called John and come from her home town. I might just change my name by deed poll! I think that I will continue the deceit for a bit, although if she starts asking awkward questions I might have to take a crash course in being you!"

The Chinese restaurant that Geoff had chosen was on the main street leading up to the train station. It was the usual one that some of the lads went to for a treat and it was upstairs above the shops. I hadn't been to any Chinese restaurants as they were a fairly new arrival both in the city and in my home town.

Waiting in Line

We arrived a minute or so before 7.30. There was no sign of Hayley so we stood talking about his favourite football team, Chelsea. I wasn't a big football fan but had been to see Leeds United at Elland Road with Jack Charlton and Billy Bremner in the team.

With England winning the World Cup last year, football attendances had been boosted as a so-called legacy of holding the tournament in England. There had been a number of matches in the north-east which had hosted the North Korean team that had done so well.

Suddenly, Hayley turned up and surprisingly by her side was Jenny. Hayley explained that since they were new to the city, Jenny had helped her find the Chinese restaurant. It seemed a bit far-fetched but, much to Geoff's dismay, I made the most of it.

"Do you fancy having a meal Jenny and making a foursome?"

She jumped at the chance but Hayley looked a little dismayed.

"We could go somewhere else Jenny, if you want." I said trying to find a compromise for all concerned.

"No, having a foursome will be great, won't it Hayley?"

"Yes, of course." Hayley replied, seemingly without much enthusiasm.

"So it's settled," Jenny confirmed and the four of us entered the door and climbed the stairs. As we did I whispered to Geoff. "Remember you are John and I am Alan!"

"OK," he said, "and I'm from Yorkshire!"

EVA

We didn't see Alan or anyone we knew the next weekend and we stood in the cold night air for two hours each night with no selection at all. We were getting a bit fed up with the sexism of 1967 but thought that we would give it one more try before returning 'home'.

Standing in line the following Saturday we both saw Alan crossing the bridge with a cute guy, slightly taller than Alan. We looked at each other and Joy said in her usual forthright manner. "You'd better have the gorgeous looking one as it might be John. I'll take Alan off so you can get in there."

"Thanks Joy ….. I mean Jenny!"

Alan walked straight up to us. "Hi Jenny, hi Hayley. This is John and he comes from Castleford so maybe he's the one you want. Here you are John; these are your cousins."

"Hi." Said John seeming a bit nervous. I took no chances and grabbed him by the arm, maybe a bit too forcefully but I had found my man, my John from the 17th century and he looked just as gorgeous as I thought he would. I had done it! Mission accomplished! But I had to be careful not to give anything away. I'm Hayley. I'm Hayley I repeated under my breath.

John still looked a bit nervous and unsure but it might have been my forthright approach in grabbing his arm. Maybe the girls of 1967 weren't as forward. Alan and Jenny followed and the two boys signed us in. Once inside, Alan and Jenny disappeared down the stairs leaving John and I alone. He was seriously cute but seemed reluctant to talk, so I made all the running.

"Which part of Castleford do you live in?" Of course I knew the answer to this question. He lived in the house that I was living in!

"Er... the Leeds side." He said to my surprise. Maybe his family had moved when his Nanna Eva had died in 1963. I had to be cautious though. Not too many questions.

"Whereabouts do you live, Hayley?" He asked.

"Ferry Fryston." There was no reason at this time in his life for him to know that but later he would.

"Whereabouts is that?" This was a strange question for him to ask and with that accent. Clearly it wasn't a Yorkshire accent. He had lived in Ferry Fryston at some point, in my house!

"Are you having a joke with me?"

"Yes, I suppose I am." He smiled. "Where are you staying now is what I meant to say."

"Hallgarth Street. Number 53. We've rented a house for a bit from a Mr Fewings."

"How long do you plan to stay here?"

"Until the A Level results come out, then I'm off to uni."

"Uni. Where's that?"

"University silly. You are a bit of a joker aren't you?"

"Yes, a bit. Which university do you hope to go to?"

"Probably Leeds, so I can stay with my parents rather than get student accommodation. It's cheaper if you stay at home rather than paying thousands of pounds on renting accommodation. I know that you can get loans and pay it off later when you have a job but it is still a millstone around your neck, being in debt."

John gave me a strange look. "But that's a lot of money for just renting accommodation. Thousands of pounds you say. John er…I mean Alan gets a full grant because his parents aren't well off and that's only £360 per annum to cover all hall costs, tuition fees and all other costs."

I realised my inflationary mistake!

"My parents are rich so that's why they pay for everything and then they're going to make me pay the money back to them when I get a job." I lied.

"But that won't be thousands of pounds will it?"

"No, I must have exaggerated a bit. What course are you doing?"

"Economics. I'd like to go into politics or into the city perhaps like my father."

"Leeds?"

"No." He laughed. "London."

"I don't really do politics. Ever since Margaret Thatcher became Prime Minister, my dad says politics is about keeping the working class in its place and making the rich richer. Like all those bankers that get big bonuses every year

Waiting in Line

when they don't deserve it. 'Bankers' is not quite the name he uses for them."

"Sorry, Margaret who?"

Another oops!

"Oh, let's not talk about politics. What do your parents do?"

"My father is a merchant banker!"

Double oops!

Perhaps it wasn't a good idea putting bankers in the same category as politicians!

This wasn't going well. I wasn't being careful enough.

"What does your father do?" John asked.

Careful! The truthful answer was that he was a miner until the impact of the closures brought about by Maggie Thatcher started in the 1980s. I needed a proper 'posh' profession. Think Eva think!

"He runs an antique shop and my mother is a teacher." I was getting too good at this lying thing. I wanted all this conversation to stop and the best way to do that was to kiss him and that is exactly what I did!

To say that it took him by surprise might be a bit of an understatement, but it did the trick. His lips were just as luscious as I thought they would be, but despite the fact he must have thought I was a real hussy, he responded in kind.

"Shall we go down to the dance?" I asked as we came up for air.

"Yes," he stammered. It was as if he had never been kissed like that before and maybe I was a bit rough with my tongue! I held his hand as we descended the steps to the dance hall.

"What grades do you need for Leeds University?" He said trying to bring our relationship back to the social kind rather than the animalistic.

"I need 360 points to do media studies." I kissed him again forcefully before he had the chance to ask about points and media studies. What an idiot I am!

The passionate kiss seemed to do the trick again, but it didn't seem the right thing in kissing him every time I made a time travelling mistake! Why was I kissing a guy I had met when I was eleven and then again at the age of thirteen when he was sixty! Yuk! Surely he will remember me and the kisses. I tried to put that thought right out of my mind.

We got to the dance hall and I dragged him up for a dance. He seemed reluctant at first, but since it was a slow dance, eventually he didn't seem to mind. The Tremeloes were singing a song I had heard my dad play, 'Silence is Golden'. How true!

We bumped into Alan and Joy after the gig had finished and they seemed to have got on well.

"Jenny floored Jim Durrant," was the way Alan greeted John, "you should have seen it. Right hook followed by knee to crotch. It was brilliant."

"It wasn't that violent." Joy protested.

"We heard a bit of a commotion at the far end of the dance floor but thought nothing of it."

Waiting in Line

We kissed the boys goodnight (I was a little too embarrassed to do it as passionately as before in front of Joy). John asked me if he could walk me home but I said it wasn't far. In fact, Hallgarth Street was the left hand fork at the corner that included 'Sweaty Bettys' fish and chip shop and on the right Church Street, all on the opposite side of the road to Dunelm House. Alan and Joy walked towards the bridge and had another goodnight kiss.

John turned to me. "I really enjoyed tonight Hayley. Can I see you again on Monday, there's no rugby training?"

"Yes, of course."

"Can I perhaps take you for a meal? Do you like Chinese food?"

"Yes, I love Chinese food."

"It's a date then. Monday night at about 7.30."

"If there's a problem, call my mobile, it's 0 7 7 3 7….. er."

He looked blank and I smiled weakly and yes, kissed him again, hoping it would make him forget what I had said. It worked.

I waved at Joy and soon we were arm in arm discussing the night's events as we walked home.

The boys departed in the opposite direction across the bridge towards their college nearer the centre of town.

JOY

"I'm meeting John again on Monday. We're going for a Chinese." Eva said as we chatted on the way back from our evening at the dance. She was clearly very excited. "I made a bit of a fool of myself."

She explained about the mistakes that she had made. "Me too! Got into a real tangle with the A level exams. Said I was waiting for my exam results when it's only April here and we wouldn't have even taken them yet!"

"Well, we'll have to be more careful," Eva replied. "Although there's something wrong with John. I think in his youth he was a bit of a joker. He puts on a totally posh accent which is certainly not a Yorkshire one and he pretends not to know anything about Castleford."

"Maybe he's just moved there from the south."

"Maybe, but he says his father works as a banker in London."

"He could have been to a boarding school like Queen Elizabeth Grammar School in Wakefield." I ventured.

"That's not the impression I got of him when he was sixty. Anyway, let's forget it for now. I need a good night's sleep after all the excitement."

Waiting in Line

We arrived at 53, Hallgarth Street and soon I was fast asleep.

We didn't join the line on Sunday. No real need. We had found what Eva wanted. As Eva got ready for her date with John on Monday evening she turned to me with a serious expression on her face. "Will you come with me?"

"Why? John won't want both of us on a date."

"Well, I'm a bit nervous. Something's not quite right but I can't work out what. I laid awake for a couple hours last night trying to work out just what was troubling me."

"OK, I'll walk you to the Chinese restaurant and then leave you when John turns up."

She really did look stunning when she had finally finished all her make-up.

"If he doesn't fall for you, he's not the kind of man you want."

"I don't want him! He marries someone called Ann."

"Well, what do you want? You've taken all this trouble to meet him and now you don't know why."

"That's what kept me awake last night. Why am I doing this? It was initially just a thought that kept recurring and then I got totally taken up with it. I haven't thought this through have I?"

"No, not really. Anyway, go and have a good time on a date that you'll remember for the rest of your life and then we'll disappear into thin air, back from where we came."

"Yes, that's it; a night to remember."

"Oh, and no funny stuff. We wouldn't want you to take anything back to the 21st century that was conceived in the 1960s!"

She smiled and slapped me on the shoulder. "You dirty minded girl! I'm not that type of woman."

We left the house a little earlier than we had planned because Eva wanted to get there in plenty of time. We stood on the opposite side of the street from where the Chinese restaurant was situated. We were a least ten minutes early and tried to hide ourselves so as to still be able to see when John arrived. It was a couple of minutes before 7.30 by my watch when we saw them.

"Alan's come with him." I exclaimed.//
"Why's he done that?" Eva was clearly disappointed. "It will spoil everything!"//
"OK, leave it to me," I said as we walked across the road to meet them.

Alan's point of view?

It was Monday so the restaurant was quite empty.

"A table for four please." Geoff said in a very posh 'I'm familiar to this sort of dining' manner, "and could we have the à la carte menu please?"

Jenny looked at Hayley in a way that said she was impressed, however, Hayley's look was a perplexed one.

"This way, sir." The waiter was seemingly impressed in the same way that Jenny was. Geoff's forthrightness probably took him by surprise too as it wasn't a particularly posh place to eat.

We sat down with Jenny opposite me and Hayley to her left, Geoff to my right. Boys vs Girls! There was a silent few minutes as we perused the menus that the waiter had promptly brought to us. We were all probably trying to make out what the options were, at least I was. Some words like 'curry' were OK but what the hell was a 'Foo Yung'.

The waiter returned. Despite his disappointment at not being alone with Hayley, Geoff took control as I floundered.

"I'll have the Duckling à l' Orange and could I have the rice with it."

The girls had no problem in choosing. "I think I'll have the Chicken Chow Mein and the chips option please," Jenny said confidently.

"Yes, I'll have the King Prawn Fried Rice please." Hayley was equally as confident.

They all looked at me. I hadn't a clue what to say and found myself saying, "I'd like to try something a little different." I addressed the waiter. "What is a Chicken Foo Yung?"

"It's an omelette." Came the reply from Geoff, Jenny and Hayley in unison.

"I'll have that with the chips option then please."

The girls giggled and Geoff smiled a sympathetic smile. Even the waiter had a smile on his face as he left with our order. At least my lack of sophistication had lightened the atmosphere a little!

"He's forgotten the drinks," said Geoff. "What do you two ladies want?"

"Could we have two wine spritzers?" Jenny replied without giving Hayley any choice.

Geoff called the waiter back. "The ladies would like two wine spritzers and we want two pints of lager."

The waiter looked as blank as Geoff and I looked.

"Wine spritzer?" He repeated in a quizzical non-Yorkshire accent.

"Yes, it's a white wine and soda water drink in a long glass." Jenny helped the waiter out.

The waiter nodded, although I was not sure he understood. We would find out shortly.

"Is it like a wine shandy?" I asked.
"Yes, sort of," said Jenny.

The conversation turned to rugby and it turned out that the girls were avid Rugby League supporters and thought it was a better game than Rugby Union. A discussion then ensued about the merits of both codes.

For some reason Hayley seemed to go very quiet as if something had dawned on her or she was thinking hard about something that had been said.

"Which school did you go to John?" she asked.

Before I could help Geoff out with the answer to Hayley's question, he replied without thinking.

"Haberdasher Aske."
I saw Hayley's face drop. "Where's that?"
Geoff realized what he'd said. "In Leeds," he said hastily.
"I don't think it is," came Hayley's accusation.

Geoff looked at me as if for help. I couldn't think of anything to say that would help.

At exactly the wrong moment, despite Jenny trying to lighten the mood, Jeanette and Andrew walked into the restaurant.

"Hi Geoff, hi John." They greeted us as they would normally do. Both girls looked at me.

"It's just a pet name," was the only thing I could think of.

At this point Hayley ran out of the room in tears. Geoff followed her leaving myself and Jenny not knowing what to do and a very surprised Jeanette and Andrew wondering what they had done wrong to have sparked such a reaction.

Eva

As I got ready for my date with John, I was excited. We had had a strange first meeting, but I had made a number of mistakes, which may have thrown him a little. Joy said I looked lovely but she would wouldn't she. Compared to her I thought that I was a dull unattractive girl. I decided to ask her if she would come with me as I was a bit nervous of walking there on my own. After a moment's deliberation she said she would.

In truth, my nervous state was far more than just being worried about walking there on my own. For the first time I began to doubt that what I was doing was sensible. There was something not right about John. I had a sort of vision of what he would be like and the kind of eyes he would have, but neither of these seemed to be right. Yes, people can change their accent and the way they speak depending on how long they live in a certain area, but he had never once mentioned living in London or that his dad was a posh banker. I'm pretty certain that he said his dad was a miner like mine. However, Joy as ever had a solution to my doubts.

"You haven't thought this through have you?" She had said followed by, "just treat it as a very special date that you'll remember for the rest of your life and hopefully John won't! We can then disappear back from where we came!"

I agreed and we left it at that.

We arrived slightly early and chose to stand in the shadows across the street from the restaurant. I was incredibly nervous even though I had met John a number of times before in my life, this was very different. Was this really what I wanted?

Joy and I were surprised when both Alan and John turned up. "What are we going to do?" I asked Joy.

"Have a foursome," came the predictable reply. I was unsure. On one hand having Joy there would make me less nervous. She would take centre stage and let me be more myself and I would not have to try and force the conversation and then make daft mistakes. On the other hand, this was supposed to be my dream date.

We walked across the street and before I had chance to make up my mind, Joy had jumped at Alan's suggestion of a double date. The date started well enough. John kissed me on both cheeks, French-style, and although Alan found it difficult to choose something, John was in complete control as if he had done this many times. This did surprise me a little since, when John was in his sixties, he didn't appear to have the level of sophistication that he now showed at the age of eighteen.

Joy and I made a mistake in ordering the drinks. Apparently, nobody had heard of wine spritzers which made you light-headed a bit quicker (for some reason) than just a glass of wine.

It was something that John said as we ate our meals that worried me. We were talking about the difference between Rugby League and Rugby Union. It seemed to surprise John that we were keen Rugby League fans. He said that he didn't realize girls liked rugby and then he said, "I've never played Rugby League, we only played Rugby Union at my school."

When I asked him which school he went to, he gave me a strange name I'd never heard of and I was certain when I first met 'my John' he had said that he had played Rugby League like my dad did as well as Rugby Union at the local Grammar School.

Other things began to come back to me as Joy started to 'rabbit on' about her favourite players, who incidentally had never been born at this point in time, but thankfully neither boy picked up on it.

Many thoughts were buzzing in my head. My John's dad wasn't a merchant banker, the accent was all wrong without a trace of Yorkshire in it, his lack of knowledge of his home town or where he lived and of Rugby League which was a corner stone of anyone's knowledge if they lived in Castleford.

THIS WASN'T MY JOHN!

At this point two friends of Alan's came into the restaurant and used different names to greet them! This was the final straw in my dream date. We had been lied to. Taken for a ride. I ran.

Outside it was starting to rain. I hesitated which way to go. Suddenly a voice said, "Are you OK Hayley?"

I turned round and there was John or Geoff or whatever name he was known by.

"You pair of liars." I screamed, so loud it turned the heads of those passing by. He just stood there taking all the abuse I could hurl at him. Those passing by now looked shocked and I burst into tears.

"I'm sorry," the boy said, "when John asked me to act as if I was him I didn't think it would upset you so much. You worried him by your questions and I owed him a favour."

"You made me look a fool. Go away. I hate you."

"Sorry," he repeated his apology and walked away and that was the last I ever saw of him.

I made my way back to our digs and waited for Joy.

JOY

The foursome went really well up to a point. Alan didn't seem to know what a 'Foo Yung' was so we told him and the waiter had never heard of wine spritzers but otherwise it seemed to be a great evening. I suppose I talked a bit too much, I always do when I am nervous. Although he wasn't quite as good-looking as John, I had really fallen for Alan and I think that was making me nervous. He was all I had ever wanted in a boy, thoughtful, humorous, liked rugby, cute and slightly vulnerable, even if he didn't know what a Foo Yung was! The meal was nice although slightly blander than those I had eaten in 2013.

I had sensed that Eva had gone quiet but she often did. I suppose she couldn't get a word in edgeways and maybe was sulking a little about me agreeing to a foursome, but the massive tantrum she threw even took me by surprise.

Some friends of John's had just walked in as I was saying how much I liked Danny Orr as a player and that Hayley and I went to the 'Jungle' every time Cas were at home, when she just screamed and ran out of the room. John followed her out, supposedly to find out what her problem was. That left Alan and I alone which was great for me because I really did fancy him. John was alright and maybe slightly more cute in looks than Alan but he was really up himself and far too posh for me. Even if he was from Castleford!

A few minutes later John appeared again. He seemed agitated and aimed his aggression at poor Alan.

"I'll see you later."

"What about the bill?" Alan replied.

"I'll settle it up but that is my debt paid, understood?"

"Yes, of course."

"What was that all about?" I asked when John had gone to pay the bill.

"Nothing. He owed me a favour and now it's paid up fully. What do you fancy doing now?"

"Snogging you!" Probably not the right thing to say but a girl must lead from the front to get what she wants!

"What?"

"Sorry, I mean shall we go to the Student Union for a drink or is there a quieter pub somewhere?"

"There's the Angel."

"That sounds perfect," and we left for the Angel.

The pub wasn't too far away and he put his arm around me as we sheltered under his umbrella and walked as quickly as we could. Once inside the pub, Alan put his umbrella in the stand by the door, we took off our wet coats and hung them up and then he went to the bar and bought the drinks. I offered to pay for them but he said it was the man's job to pay for everything. I liked the sound of that! I was a bit more traditional with my drink in the pub and went for a lager and lime, pint of, which did surprise him a bit. I loved the ambience in the pub; it was what I would call, once again, quaint. We sat there in a dark corner of what Alan had called the 'snug' and chatted about our futures. I think that he said it was called a 'snug'. At least I hoped that's what he said and it wasn't a request to 'snog' him! For the first time I noticed how white his teeth were when he smiled, how his blue eyes glistened and how smooth his complexion was with no foundation cream or it might just have been because the 'snug' was badly lit.

The pub was nearly empty and it felt quite romantic, as we sat there in the dim light hand in hand. He was in my book gorgeous and I definitely was falling in love with him. It's funny how women just know they are in love whereas with men it takes just a little bit longer, but soon he would know that he was in love with me!

He put his arm around me again, and although Alan didn't like the word, we 'snogged' or to put it in his terms had a passionate lingering kiss which sent tingles right through me.

I did feel a little guilty for Eva but hey! Every woman for herself I thought as I snuggled closer to Alan.

"Do you think Hayley will be alright?"
"Yes, of course. Tantrums come and go. The sad thing for you men is that you can't have a teary tantrum like us women without being called a wuss or gay."
"Gay. What's that?"
"Being happy like I am at this moment," and I kissed him passionately again which seemed to be the best way of getting myself out of yet another sticky situation.

We finished our first, or was it second drinks quite quickly and Alan returned to the bar for 'same again'. When he got back with the drinks he looked worried.

"Look, there's something I ought to tell you."
"You're married?"
"No." He smiled, all eyes and teeth again.
"You have another girlfriend at home?"
"No, will you let me explain Miss 'Talkative'? I haven't been totally honest with you."
"You're gay?"
"Yes, I'm happy enough. Listen, my name isn't Alan, it's John. When I first met you, for some reason, you kept asking me lots of questions. Was I called John? Where was I from? I'm afraid I kind of freaked out and told you a lie. Then, because Geoff owed me a favour, I got him to pretend that he was me. That is, he was called John and came from Yorkshire, whereas the truth is he's called Geoff and he's from London. Couldn't you tell by the accent?"
"Yes, I guess Hayley and I both noticed that. Two questions though; Why did Geoff owe you a favour? And why on earth would you want him to impersonate you?"
"You really don't want to know what I did for him to owe me a favour, but in answer to your second question, you scared me and I wanted you off my case. Sounds silly now, feeling the way I do about you."
"What way is that Alan ... sorry John. It's going to take a bit of getting used to!"
"I really like you. I think you are one beautiful sexy lady."
"Well thank you, kind sir, you are not so bad yourself but I too have a confession."
"You're married or what was that other word, …. gay?"

"No, neither, but I'm not called Jenny, I'm called Joy."
"Why the name change?"
"It's a long story but shall we just say that Hayley, who is in fact called Eva, and I wanted to go incognito."

That might have been a mistake to divulge Eva's name but this could not be her John because, as Eva had said, he marries a girl called Ann and I might be marrying this guy!

We had a few more pints and I was waiting for John to 'try it on' on the way back to Hallgarth Street, but it never happened. I was half hoping it would. I'd never been treated with such courtesy before. Twenty-first century lads would have tried something on and got a slap for their pains, but John did nothing but kiss me with his soft lips as tenderly as I've ever been kissed. In time, he would surely get round to it. I thought 1967 boys with all their 'flower power' and free love would be up for a bit of 'desert's disease' or 'roving palms' as we girls knew it, but not my John. We kissed again, one long lingering kiss and then we said our goodnights.

And without thinking I said it for the first time ever. "I love you."
"I love you too," he replied.

GEOFF

It was raining as I rushed out of the restaurant in pursuit of Hayley. I found her stood just outside, crying. She screamed something at me and I said that I was sorry. She seemed to have a lot of pent up anger and most of the people passing by gave me strange looks. I partially deserved being screamed at since Hayley had clearly seen through my lies and John's. I couldn't find the right words that would have made it any better. Whatever I had said at that moment would have come over as childish and what we had done was downright childish.

She walked off towards the city centre and sadly that was the last I ever saw of her.

I met John the next day at training. He thanked me for a wonderful evening. I could have punched him but I was as much to blame as he was.

He kept talking about some girl he'd met called Joy. It didn't make any sense to me but he was clearly smitten by her. He went on and on about how they'd kissed. I tried to explain my humiliation in the street at the hands of a very irate Hayley, but he wasn't interested.

Waiting in Line

Finally, he said. "There's a moral to all this Geoff, my friend: however much fun it seems at the time, always be yourself."

I hit him hard!

EVA

It was really late when Joy got back home that night and I was beginning to worry. She was singing and laughing and obviously had had a bit too much to drink as she crashed through the front door. I wasn't in the mood for all her drunken antics so I went to bed.

The next morning, I decided to tell Joy that we were leaving. I had had enough of 1967 and wanted to go and buy tickets for our return to Beverley. The one thing I thought she might want to do was spend the £400 or so that we still had remaining from our winnings. Maybe I could start the antique shop I had always thought about, by buying artefacts from 1967 and selling them in 2013.

Joy was in one of her 'joyous' periods so I left it for a couple of days as she seemed to be enjoying herself with that two-faced rat-bag of a boy called Alan or was it John?

I never wanted to see his ugly mug again and was really regretting getting involved with nineteen sixty flaming seven!

I went shopping in the city centre to keep myself occupied and see if I could get any bargains in the market.

Joy had agreed to split the money 50-50 and so I had about £200 to spend minus a bit more rent, food and of course travel expenses back to Beverley.

I bought a couple of beige suede miniskirts which were very short, some skinny-ribbed purple jumpers and a dozen 'flower power' blouses. I wasn't too sure what might sell well in 2013 but lashed out on some vinyl records of original Beatles' long playing records or LPs as they called them. I bought 30 copies of the 'Sergeant Pepper's Lonely Hearts Club Band' LP over the next week. I think they thought I was mad but I knew how much they would go for in pristine condition in 2013. I also bought some Rolling Stones' and Four Seasons' records and 30 copies of another LP I'd heard my dad talk about; 'Pet Sounds' by the Beach Boys. He said that it was the best LP ever made.

I was enjoying my spending spree but I knew I was putting off the moment when I had to tell Joy that we were leaving. As that day grew closer for we had been in 1967 for nearly a month, I made my final purchase; a new large case to put all my other purchases in!

As I arrived home carrying my nearly empty suitcase, Joy was sitting in the front room awaiting my arrival. She was in a sombre mood and I thought that maybe her love affair with the lying John had come to a tragic end because, as I hoped, he had confessed about having another girl that he was engaged to. How spiteful could I be!

"Hi Eva. Been busy shopping again?"
"Yes, I needed something to take all this stuff back in. I'm going to make a small fortune with all this lot. You really

ought to do the same but I think they may have run out of Beatles' and Beach Boys' records. Dusty Springfield records might be a good bet though or Lulu's. I think they do have a bit of a comeback with Take That."

"Listen, I've got something to tell you. Please sit down Eva."

I did as I was told.

JOY

Although I couldn't bring myself to tell Eva just yet, I had decided that I never wanted to return with her to 2013. I hated my life back then. Despite my name and the way that I acted, I hated it. I had made plans without ever saying anything to Eva and when I met John it only confirmed what I wanted to do with my life. I loved 1967, although of course I hadn't known this for certain when I had left 2013. 1967 had a simplicity, a less frantic way of living, no mobiles telling people where you were, no constant receiving of texts and no CCTV monitoring your every move. Yes, you couldn't book holidays on-line and actually had to go to a travel-agent to do it and maybe travelling to far off places was a little more difficult, but there was a beauty and innocence to 1967, even if I hadn't seen much evidence of 'flower power', free love or drugs in Durham. 1967 was definitely a less dangerous time than 2013 with all its terrorist suicide bombers and horrific murders and stabbings.

The run up to my A level examinations had been a nightmare. My parents constantly argued and were set to divorce. The boys of 2013 had no manners or morals. Here in 1967 they had both and in John there was a degree of gentleness and kindness that I had not seen before. Life was of a slower pace but at least with having John, I would never have to 'wait in line' for a dance ever again. The music was far better than anything in 2013. I hadn't heard much in the way of swearing in the month I had been here. No effing or blinding with every other word.

The one thing that I had done to ensure that my life from now on was going to be a rich and prosperous one was, no not John, you never know how long relationships last, it was that I had cut out some of the pages of dad's big book for 1967 right up to the end of 1999 and I had made a comprehensive list of all the major sporting results. The teacher that said 'information is power' was right and I had all the information I needed to make a fortune. I had every result you could wish to have: every cup final, election result, Grand National winner and not to mention the knowledge of what devices to invest in to make money. I was going to be very rich, something that was far from certain in 2013. In fact, I was going to be very, very rich! I could bet with certainty on everything and what's more make right decisions as far as stocks and shares were concerned, and I haven't even mentioned the winning lottery ticket numbers I had researched with the help of Camelot!! The future looked very Joyful!

Eva didn't take my decision to remain in 1967 very well. In fact, that was a bit of an understatement. She went ballistic.

"What about your parents? Your brothers and sisters? Your career? Your A level results. What about me? You cannot expect me to come back and fetch you!" Her rant went on.

"I blame myself. I should never have told you what I was going to do and should never ever have allowed you to come with me!"

As her rant began to peter out, I offered my reasons for staying.

"Don't be stupid! They're going to suss you out and fling you in jail and throw away the key! Don't you think a bookie isn't going to get a tad suspicious when every time you bet on anything it comes up trumps?"

"I'll be careful. Spread my bets. Advise others for a fee. There are lots of options. I am intelligent, but the one thing I will miss more than anything Eva is you. You have been a good friend but now, thanks to you, I know what I want and that is to remain here in 1967."

We hugged each other. Both of us were in tears.

"If that's what you want Joy," she said quietly, "then that's the way it must be. I can always come back and see how you're getting on."
"Would you do that for me?"
"Yes, of course!"

JOHN

I received a letter from my mum saying that my grandfather, Tom, had died and asking me if I could make the funeral at All Saints Church in Castleford. Tom had been a real stalwart of the church. He and his wife Eva, and my parents Pearl and Harry, between them, had run the small mission church of St James since the 1920s. Tom had been the writer of plays and pantomimes performed at the church, which could act as a church hall as well as a place of worship. Tom had even acted in some of the plays and his sketch on 'Is this the way to Wareham?' was legendry. Now he was gone to join his beloved sweet wife, Nanna Eva. They had moved up to Yorkshire from the wonderful Forest of Dean, from a town called Cinderford to be exact, so that Tom could work as a 'plate layer' for a mining corporation.

I packed a small bag of mostly washing for mum to do and set off to walk the two and a half miles to Durham station. Hitching was out of the question as I was still having problems with my hand injury. I was really missing playing rugby but such is fate and I guess the cow wasn't too pleased, wherever it was.

Waiting in Line

I walked down the lane and out on to the road towards the city centre. The route took me down Hallgarth Street, passed 'Sweaty Bettys' fish and chip shop and over Dunelm bridge into Palace Green by the Cathedral and then down to the city centre and finally up to the station at the top of the hill. The views from the station or from the train over the city were magnificent and were always a welcome sight.

As I reached the top of Hallgarth Street, there was a young woman, presumably a student, dragging a rather large case out of a house. She was really struggling.

"Don't I know you from somewhere?" I asked as I approached her. "Do you want a hand with that case?"

She turned and after a moment said, "Yes, you are the one Joy and I met at York station. You've still got your hand in a bandage I see."

"Yes, afraid so. It had to be re-broken and hasn't mended quite right yet. I can still give you a hand with that case though. I've become ambidextrous!"

"Thanks. I can take your bag in return."

"It's a deal. Where are you going?"

"To the station."

"What a coincidence, so am I."

She looked at me in a strange way that was hard to interpret as if she was trying to work something out. Then she gave a beaming smile but said nothing.

We walked on and chatted. She had decided to leave Durham University; I think she said she was at St Mary's but had found life away from home too difficult to deal with, as many students did.

"Where are you headed?" I asked.

"First to York then to Beverley."

"I've never been to Beverley. It has a race course doesn't it and a Minster?"

"Yes, it has both. And where are you going?"

"Sad thing really, I'm going home to the funeral of my grandfather, Tom."

"That is sad. Where is the funeral taking place?"

"I live in a mining town called Castleford. Have you heard of it? It's famous for two things; a sculptor called Henry Moore and its Rugby League team, Castleford Tigers."

Again she gave me a beaming smile. "Oh yes, I've heard of Castleford. Which church is the funeral at?"

"Tom and his wife Eva ran a small mission church called St James' but it's very small and there will be a lot at the funeral so they've moved it to a sister church called All Saints about a mile away in Hightown."

She giggled and then laughed out loud which seemed a strange response to my comments about Tom's funeral.

"Can we sit together on the train?" She asked.

"Well, as far as York I suppose then we'll have different connections."

I turned to face her and I am sure I heard her whisper something very strange.

It sounded like. '**Thank you, Nanna Eva**'.